i

SPECIAL PROPER MAGIC
by Michael McAdam

ISBN 978-1-7781190-1-9

This novel is entirely a work of fiction. The names, characters and incidents portrayed in it are the work of the author's imagination. Any resemblance to actual persons, living or dead, events or localities is entirely coincidental.

Cover and interior illustrations by M.J. San Juan.

Michael McAdam asserts the moral right to be identified as the author of this work. For more information, follow @twogargs on Twitter or see twogargs.com

For Sherri

"I have found both freedom and safety in my madness; the freedom of loneliness and the safety from being understood, for those who understand us enslave something in us."
—Kahlil Gibran

ACKNOWLEDGEMENTS

I want to thank The Muse Herself, **Sherri W.**, for being the reason I persevered and kept writing this book, discovering new things along the journey; **Susan G.** for excellent edits and suggestions to positively affect my writing; **Mike R.** for being an excellent proofreader and formatter and helping me focus on hyphens; **Lisa R.**, whose excellent eye for detail brought out the best in this book's cover, and for **Marci M.**, who was there at the beginning and has read her way to the present.

Chapters

Chapter 1: The Boy

"There was a boy. A very strange, enchanted boy."
—eden ahbez

In England, in the village of Little Colchester, or more properly just outside it, was a vast, ancestral mansion owned by the Whitingham family: Locksley Hall. Legend had it that it was named for the famous Earl of Locksley, better known as Robin Hood.

For a century or more, the enormous, sprawling home had dominated the misty green countryside, giving rise to more than a few tales whispered around the village of hauntings, odd sounds heard in the night, strange lights in the distance and a general air of mystery.

It was the home of one Adrian Whitingham, the only child of that family, who after having spent the entire school year at a boys-only boarding school had come home… only to find himself alone and with nothing to do.

"You'll have to amuse yourself, I'm afraid," his father had said. "Work has me travelling, and your mother has several gallery showings on the docket, as it were." Adrian's father was a banker, an international banker as he often pointed out. Adrian thought he said it that way so he could sound more important.

Adrian's mother was a photographer, though really it was more of a jumped-up hobby than anything. Although he thought her pictures were pretty, it was her status in the community that got her attention, rather than her talent.

Adrian's parents were the well-to-do sort of socialites that nonetheless still seemed somehow boring, rather faded and lacklustre; no matter what they did, it felt as if they never really made a splash. They were quiet, proper people and truth be told, Adrian had privately nicknamed them The Grays, thinking they lived a drab existence without colour.

Adrian himself was a piercingly intelligent boy of average height with raven black hair, and his pale skin gave him a somewhat haunting look; he took great care with his clothes, every crease and tuck in exactly the right place. He was fastidious to the point of being called "fussy" by his mother.

In addition to his pallor he had another interesting trait: he had yellow eyes.

Some people may have had eyes that were amber or pale green, but Adrian's eyes were yellow like a wolf's, or perhaps a hawk's. They stood out in contrast to his otherwise silent features, giving him a striking and unsettling look when he made direct eye contact with anyone.

His friends at school called them "witch's eyes," and they had earned him the nickname of "Spooky." Far from being put off by this, thirteen-year-old Adrian found it to be rather cool.

Finally, there was a trait he possessed which was somewhat less obvious: Adrian could move things with his mind. His mother and father did not know he could do this. Even at his age, Adrian knew such inexplicable things were considered too strange even for him, and wanted to avoid any awkward, unpleasant questions.

It had begun at school, where he had stood a pencil on its point during a boring moment in class, and it had not fallen down. In fact, as long as he kept looking at it, it continued to stand. Once he'd looked away, it toppled over as it should have done.

He'd experimented, to see if it was all really *real*, and had been able to move the pencil from one side of the desk to the other just by thinking about it.

It had been difficult to find time alone to practice this talent while at school, since there were always people about, but he would find quiet places like the library or the chapel and try his ability there. He found he could move books, lamps; open and close doors and windows; he could move anything smaller than a trunk, it seemed.

Keeping this trait of his a secret wasn't hard, given that he didn't have many friends at school, and risking them blabbing about his gift to the entire school couldn't be tolerated—and thus, Adrian had kept silent about it.

But now that it was summer break, Adrian was looking forward to some private time where he would finally be able to practice his gift uninterrupted. He had even Googled the ability and the name for it: *telekinesis*. He loved saying it to himself; it made his ability sound all the more special.

He wondered where it had come from; no one else in the family seemed to have it, or perhaps like himself, they weren't telling? In any case, it made him feel unique and perhaps just a little bit isolated. It was one thing, of course, to be special and have an ability no one else had; it was quite another to be able to do something other people weren't likely to understand.

Adrian decided that he was all right with this; he already felt different than others, alone and apart from them in many respects, from being intelligent (it always amazed him how other boys didn't want to appear "too brainy" or reveal how smart they were) to just generally keeping to himself.

"Shy" wasn't the right word for it; he simply preferred being alone. He was perfectly capable of handling conversations with people his own age, or even adults; it was simply that most times he chose not to. He liked the quiet, and enjoyed the solitude of his own company.

Which meant, with his parents busy and out of the picture (*"You'll have to amuse yourself,"* indeed!), he anticipated having loads of time to unlock his gift's secrets.

That is, until the mansion's front doorbell rang. He wasn't to understand until later just how much his life was about to change.

Chapter 2: The Girl

"From childhood's hour I have not been as others were; I have not seen as others saw."
—Edgar Allan Poe

Holly sighed as she stared out the window of the train, rain streaming down the glass pane as the scenery—a series of towns and villages—rolled by. Mom and Dad had surprised her with a summer trip to England—without even talking to her about it first.

Her father, Nathan Weaver, was a scientist with his own laboratory in their huge house in Boston, Massachusetts. Her mother Olivia was, too, and in fact they'd first met at some big science convention—he was presenting a piece on genetics and she had published a paper on Evolution Theory and they hit it off immediately.

Lately, it seemed that science was more important than their only daughter, and they had made plans to go to

England for the entire summer to do research or some other such reason, and were simply packing her along with them.

Like many thirteen year old girls, Holly wondered sometimes if her parents had a clue—any clue at all. Did they not understand that losing a summer to visit boring, stodgy old England would bore her to death?

Could a person actually die from boredom? she wondered. It seemed she was going to find out.

She studied her fingernails; she had been allowed to (finally!) choose her own colour and had decided to paint them a pretty blue to match her eyes (as well as the blue of her favourite jacket that she was wearing for the trip). It was the one splash of colour in her wardrobe, as Holly favoured black jeans and long-sleeved black shirts with high collars; her mother had tried unsuccessfully to get her to enjoy dresses and colourful, more feminine apparel but Holly would have none of it.

"I'm not some kind of dress-up doll," she had told her mother. "I'm *me*." Mrs. Weaver had sighed and smiled at her. "You certainly are," she had said, stroking Holly's long, silky black hair.

"Excuse me," said a voice, interrupting Holly's reverie. "Do you know which stop is Colchester?"

Holly looked up to see a rather tired but kindly-looking woman clutching an old-fashioned brown purse, wearing a shabby brown coat and with a kerchief tied under her ample chin.

Holly looked up at the train map which was printed on the wall of the train car. Perhaps the old woman hadn't seen it.

"It's three stops from here," she said.

"Oh, bless you, dearie," said the woman.

"What was that, dear?" said her mother, looking up from her tablet.

"I was just telling the lady where her stop was," said Holly.

"What lady?" her mother asked, looking around.

Holly's eyes looked sadly into the kindly old woman's. "She's gone, Mum," she said. Holly's mother couldn't see the lady. Of course she couldn't. The lady was—as Holly now realised, looking at the age of her clothes and purse—a ghost.

Holly had been able to see and speak to ghosts for as long as she could remember; she could do it so well that most times she couldn't tell the difference between real people and the dead—another reason she hated travelling away from everything that was familiar and going to someplace new. She would have to be extra careful to make sure the people she spoke to were actually *there*.

The ghost smiled at Holly and wandered away, muttering "Colchester" to herself.

Holly sighed; Colchester was their stop, too. Hers and her parents'. What were the odds the one ghost she'd talked to so far was going to the exact same place she was? They always seemed to follow her around; no matter where she went, the dead seemed to find her, like she was some kind of ghost magnet.

It was *annoying*.

She had learned the hard way to be quiet, to be careful no one saw her talking to "people that weren't there," because everyone at school called her "Ghost Girl" ever since she'd been caught talking to a ghost when she was younger, and had not known any better than to tell the truth—which of course no one believed.

And now she was going to be cooped up in some stuffy old English house with some cousin she'd never met, and would have to watch herself or he'd think she was a freak just like everyone else did.

What kind of name was Adrian, anyway? He was probably some wheezy little kid whose only interest was toy trains and custard creams or whatever English kids were into.

She sighed as the train pulled into Colchester station. This was going to be the worst summer *ever*.

Chapter 3: The First House

"Houses are like people—some you like and some you don't like—and once in a while there is one you love."
—L.M. Montgomery

Locksley Hall, when her family pulled up in the car they'd rented, was both incredibly cool to Holly and also somehow annoying—what kind of family needed a house that was practically a castle? It was so big you could put eight families in it and still have plenty of rooms left over.

Her father explained that it was an old manor house, and in those days well-to-do people had a virtual army of servants and any number of relatives coming and going, and so the houses back then had to be large enough to fit the circumstances of the families that lived in them.

"There are homeless people in the world. One family doesn't need all this space," Holly groused.

"Dear, don't be difficult." Her mother said. Her mother was always saying that, it seemed. "We live in a big house, too." Which was true.

But it isn't crazy English two-century-old-looking big like Locksley Hall! Holly thought. *And what if I am difficult? It doesn't mean it isn't true.*

Holly tried counting the windows on just one of the three floors—and wasn't able to finish before the car pulled up into the *porte-cochère*—which she had read was a fancy name for a roofed extension from the front door of a house over the driveway, so cars could park and people could get out without being rained on.

Fancy house, fancy driveway. Ugh, Holly thought. She was disliking the cousin she had never met more and more. *I bet he thinks he's fancy, too.*

Her father rang the doorbell. It was answered by a neatly dressed man with short trimmed black hair wearing a business suit. The two men shook hands and Holly was introduced to her Uncle Frederick. "You can call me 'Uncle Freddy,'" he said. (Holly didn't think she'd ever met anyone who seemed *less* like a "Freddy" than this man.)

Aunt Emily was next; as Holly received a weak hug from her, she could tell Emily was trying to seem like more of a free spirit than Frederick but clearly wasn't fully committed to the role: her dress, though flowy, was too conservative for someone who was obviously trying very hard to appear "artistic." Her hair was also cut in a short bob that looked straight out of a high-end salon. Holly tried to think charitably of her, but Holly had never been able to stand people who were fake.

Then they were invited in, and she was introduced to her cousin, Adrian.

Boy and girl sized each other up, each with suspicious, guarded looks on their faces; for Holly's part, she thought Adrian looked stuck-up in his jacket and collared shirt and skinny jeans—he looked too perfect. Also, his eyes were weird and made her feel like he was looking at her as if she were something he'd like to bite, which made her want to smack him.

Adrian, seeing the girl with raven hair and blue jacket, thought she looked nice, and rather pretty, and was prepared to give her the benefit of the doubt, until their eyes met.

He could tell right away she was smart—she looked at him with an intelligence that made him feel like she was looking through him. This made him frown.

"Hullo," he said sullenly. "I'm Adrian."

"Holly Weaver," she said. They shook hands as their parents had done.

"Excellent!" said Uncle Frederick. "Now you two have met, Adrian, why don't you show your cousin around? We'll call you when it's time for dinner."

Adrian glared at his father's back as he conducted the adult Weavers away to their rooms. His father had just dumped a stranger, cousin or not, on him for the entire afternoon. So much for privacy!

Still, Adrian remembered his manners. He asked Holly: "How was your trip?"

"Long and boring," Holly said instantly, then felt a little bad for saying it.

"Even the train?" Adrian said, and seemed surprised. Holly remembered that boys all seemed to like trains for some reason. She sighed.

"I suppose the train was interesting enough," she said. Of course, it was because she'd talked with a ghost but he didn't need to know that.

"Your house is huge," she said. She instantly hated that she'd said it. It sounded stupid to say it out loud; one thing Holly was not good at was small talk. It, too, was too fake for her.

"Want a tour?" Adrian asked.

Holly felt very much like staying in the exact spot in which she was standing until it was time to go back to Boston—but as that would have been impossible, she chose instead to say "Okay."

She followed the strange, spooky boy with the weird eyes deeper into the house, thinking the whole time that this was how scary movies always started, that the place was probably full of ghosts and she wasn't going to be able to leave England without having some kind of crazy nonsense happen to her.

As it turned out, she was right.

The house was divided into two wings, East and West. It had three floors. Adrian led Holly up the stairs to the second floor, then turned left down the West hallway.

"My parents thought you'd like the room next to mine," he said.

Holly almost said "What for?" but despite her frustration at being abandoned by her parents five seconds after they were indoors, managed to remember that Adrian was in the same boat: "Hi-this-is-your-cousin-show-her-around-bye-bye-now."

At least we have that in common, she thought.

However, her grumpiness faded somewhat when she saw the room. She had anticipated something old-world and antiquey, but the room was so much more than that: a big four poster bed, nightstand, a wardrobe, an actual dressing table and mirror, and even the lightswitch was the old kind with two buttons—one for "on" and one for "off".

There was a lovely bookshelf full of books and decorative figurines and knick-knacks that Holly thought might have been from the nineteenth century or something;

her imagination seized her as she pictured to whom they might have originally belonged.

"This room is great," she said, and she meant it.

Adrian seemed pleased. "I think so, too. Would you like some time to yourself, or shall I show you around some more?"

"Can I have both?" Holly asked, having decided not to be rude but still wanting some private time alone with her thoughts.

Adrian laughed. "Of course. My room is just next door—I'm happy just hanging out there until you feel up to continuing. I'll leave my door open."

"Thanks," said Holly.

"Not at all," Adrian said, very grown-up-host-like.

Adrian left, leaving Holly grateful that he, at least, seemed able to read her mood enough to know when to leave her alone. *That was pretty cool of him,* she decided.

She took a deep breath, enjoying her view of the extensive, green back yard (what English people called their "garden") through the rivulets of rain on her window. Rain had its own way of making her feel calm, like the world had slowed down enough to make sense.

There was a sudden knock at the door.

Holly swore to herself.

"Who is it?" she asked.

"Tea, miss?" came a woman's voice.

Holly opened the door and there stood a maid, in classic-styled English maid's uniform: a grey dress with a white apron over top, puffy sleeves, and her hair up in a bun. Holly guessed the woman was still quite young.

"Mrs. Macready marked your arrival, Miss, and wondered if you'd be wanting some tea after your long journey?"

Holly was taken aback. Did English people really still have servants? Was this an actual thing?

"I…um, yes please," said Holly, having decided that not only would it be good manners to accept the offer, but realising she was a bit hungry and was hoping "tea" included those cute little sandwiches you always saw at English teas on television.

"Very good, miss. May I ask a question?" said the maid, looking demurely down at her hands.

"Sure, go ahead." Holly said.

"Are you really all the way from America, Miss?" The maid's eyes were bright.

"I am. Boston, actually."

"Oh how very exciting, Miss! We'll do you up a proper English tea in the kitchen, though I'm sure it's not as grand as what you do in America."

Holly laughed. "If there's one thing I'm not, it's 'grand.' I'm Holly, by the way. Who are you?"

"Letitia, Miss. Please call me Letty. That's what I'm called, downstairs."

"All right, Letty," said Holly, reaching out to shake Letty's hand.

Letty gasped—and vanished.

Holly was crestfallen. *A ghost,* she thought. *Of course. I have to pay more attention to whom I'm speaking! Or my cousin and his parents are going to think I'm some kind of creep.*

She poked her head out of the open doorway into the hall; there was no one there. Adrian, for all that he was in the room adjacent, had not seemed to have heard her.

She sighed, turning back to her pleasant rainy window, only to find that set out on the dressing table was a silver tray on which was a plate of sandwiches, tiny little cakes with icing, a teapot with steam rising from it, a bowl of sugar cubes, a lemon wedge, a tiny jar of cream, and a china teacup—but for the freshness of the food, the whole ensemble looked like it was a hundred years old.

I think I might just like it here after all, she thought.

Chapter 4: The Garden

"If you have a garden and a library,
you have everything you need."
—Marcus Tullius Cicero

Later, Adrian was lying on his bed reading a book. Because his bedroom door was open, he couldn't practice moving things as he would have liked; instead, he concentrated on turning the pages of his book without touching them. That way, if Holly or anyone else appeared at his door, they wouldn't notice anything out of the ordinary.

As it happened, it was harder for him to move smaller things with precision than it was to move a larger object in a straight line—for example, he could make the books on his shelf fly from it to his hand, but turning the pages was like threading a needle. It was, as his mother would put it, *fiddly*. His concentration, therefore, was so intense that he was aware of nothing outside his book until Holly appeared in his doorway and spoke:

"Earth to Adrian, come in. Over." Holly's voice startled him. She was standing at the door, waving at him. He shook his head to clear it.

"Sorry," he said. "Really good book."

"I guess it must be, the way you were staring at it," she said. She looked at the book's cover. "Oh! I've read that series."

"You read?" Adrian seemed surprised.

"Well I'm not *illiterate*. American girls can read, you know."

"I only meant—nobody reads anymore. It's all apps and memes and online videos on their phones." Adrian shrugged.

"Bleah," Holly said, sticking out her tongue in a gagging motion. "Brain Deadeners, I call those. Phone Zombies." she held her arms stiffly out in front of her, pretending to reach for Adrian. "Braaaaaaains," she said in a guttural voice.

Adrian laughed. Holly was pleased to see that when he laughed, it was real—not some made-up "I have too many manners" fakey-polite laugh, but a really honest one. That was a point in his favour.

"So—the rest of the tour?" she asked.

Adrian smiled at her, genuinely and for the moment, he seemed unguarded. He thought for a moment, then seemed to turn shy as he asked: "Would you like to see a secret?"

Holly nodded emphatically. Something interesting to do, at last!

"Yes."

———

Adrian led her downstairs, and then down a long hallway past a huge kitchen. "We usually eat in there," he pointed out as they passed. "Though I daresay Mum and Dad will have us in the dining room tonight, now that you're here."

Holly had a brief impression of yellow walls, large windows with white trim, and rustic wooden furniture—a bright cosy kitchen, to be sure—but then they were past it and heading for a small room at the far end of the house, in which were buckets, gardening tools, an assortment of rubber boots and vinyl capes.

"Grab a pair of gloves," Adrian said, pointing over to a shelf upon which rested several pairs. "And a rain cape. It has a hood to keep your head from getting wet. And there are some wellies that should fit you, too."

"What are wellies?" Holly asked.

Adrian blushed. "Oh. Um. The boots," he said, pointing to the rubber ones. "Green or yellow. They're named for

Wellingtons, because the Duke of Wellington made the style famous, so now everyone calls them 'wellies.'"

"Everyone in England maybe," Holly said. "It's like Kleenex. They're tissues. Kleenex is a brand name. But everyone calls them Kleenex."

Adrian gave her a devilish smile. "Everyone in America, maybe."

"Ha," she said and slipped her feet into the boots. They were a bit large, but serviceable.

She noticed that Adrian also selected a yellow pair. "You don't want green?" she asked.

"I've always liked yellow. It's my favourite colour!" he said cheerily.

Holly found that rather nice, as the boys she knew at school weren't the type to admit to liking bright, cheerful colours. Her cousin, it seemed, had more to him than she had thought.

"Out the side door here, and then to your right around the corner." Adrian gestured out the small green door.

Once outside, Holly marvelled at how quaint the side of the house...*mansion*... was. It was as if all the pretence, the attitude, was for the front—but here on the side things could just be nice and practical like the little green side door. The house, like her cousin, also seemed to have different facets.

Funny how something as small as a cute door or yellow boots can change your mind about something, she thought.

Adrian followed the wall around the corner and vanished. Holly hurried to follow him, only to find once she rounded the corner that he had disappeared entirely.

Given her recent experience with Letty the ghost maid, she was not happy about this turn of events. But Adrian was real—wasn't he? She tried calling: "Adrian?"

"Hullo!" he said, from behind her.

She jumped. "Brat," she said. "Quit freaking me out."

"Sorry, but you did say you wanted to see a secret. Come over here. Stand right here. Now look at the wall. What do you see?"

"I see the wall of the house, you creep," she said grumpily.

"Okay. Now stand there. Watch," he said, and walked towards the wall. Once he was beside it, he turned to face Holly. "Are you watching?" he asked with a smile.

"Well, *obviously*," she said.

Adrian stepped to the left and vanished.

"What! What in the actual—" Holly spluttered.

Adrian reappeared. "It's so cool, isn't it? Come here, let me show you!" he said excitedly.

Holly approached him, still annoyed but now curious about how he'd managed the trick. As she got close enough to touch him, he pointed to the left. She looked—and realised that there was an archway there. Glancing to the right, she found one there as well.

The wall, as she now saw, was made of the same brick as the rest of the house but it was set a bit further back, so if you were looking straight at it, it would seem to be one uninterrupted wall—but was actually a kind of gate, really, into—

—She followed Adrian through the archway and gasped; it was a garden. A large, *proper* garden, with bushes and climbing ivy and delphiniums and other flowers she couldn't name. She realised that its wall, being made of the same stone as the house, stretched all the way around it to the point that she hadn't noticed where the side of the house ended and the garden wall began.

There were stone benches, a little table with chairs, and statues of fae creatures like fauns and winged fairies. There was even a statue of a little man riding a unicorn. It was like a magical garden out of a story book.

"Wow," she said, forgetting about feeling annoyed and switching to being impressed.

Adrian smiled shyly. "This is my secret garden. Like in the book, you know?"

Holly nodded. "I loved that book."

Adrian replied, "Me too."

Holly noticed Adrian had become shy all of a sudden—and she realised something.

"Am I the first person you've ever brought here?" she asked.

Adrian nodded. "I found it a few summers ago when I was bored and exploring. Dad said that one of the rooms of the house had probably been a nursery, and this was like a sort of playground for children, or maybe a lady's suite with its own private tea garden or some such, but there's no door from the inside any more. So you can only find it from outside, and only if you know where the part of the wall is that has the entrance."

Holly was incredibly moved by this. "This...this is a really good secret, Adrian, and I'm glad you showed it to me. Thank you."

Adrian smiled, red-faced again, and changed the subject by showing her the flowers. "I didn't know anything about gardening but I found some English Garden books and Mum and Dad bought me some seeds and things," he said.

There was a gardener, too, an older gentleman wearing a cap, some coveralls, and green rubber boots like the ones from the 'gardening room' with the green door. He smiled at Adrian's enthusiasm and nodded to Holly, busying himself at the other end of the garden.

Holly grinned. "Well, I guess it helps to have a gardener, too," she said.

"Huh?" Adrian said, inspecting the roots of one of his flower bushes.

The gardener approached. "Good day, Miss. Young master," he said.

He held out a flower to Holly—a perfect rose, delicate pink. "It's called a Wildeve," he said. "An English rose for our American visitor," and he touched the brim of his cap as she took it.

"Aw. Thanks," Holly said.

The gardener knelt down beside Adrian. "You see, young master, a touch of soap and water and those bugs will leave your roots alone! Well done, you looking that up!"

Holly inhaled the scent of her rose. The garden felt magical to her, wonderful and secret; she began to think that perhaps her cousin was like this garden—a proper brick wall outside, but inside—

Adrian stood up. "Well. That's coming along nicely— oh! Where'd you get the rose?"

Holly beamed. "From the gardener." She indicated the man, who nodded to her.

Adrian's eyes narrowed. "We don't have a gardener. And anyway the roses shouldn't be ready yet, it's only the beginning of summer," he said.

Holly froze. "But…" she began. The gardener had been talking to Adrian, about the roots…

…*Only Adrian hadn't responded.* Because he couldn't hear the man, or see him.

Darn it darn it DARN IT, she silently cursed.

"What's going on?" he asked.

Of all the things, why did it have to be a ghost here, now? It was only her first day, and now her cousin was going to think she was a freak. This, she did not need!

"Nothing, I was just joking," she said with what she hoped was a believable grin.

"So where'd you get the rose then?"

"Over—" she hoped she'd spot the rose bush in time to point at it, but there wasn't one she could see. She tried anyway: "—there. Over there somewhere."

"You know what I'm good at?" Adrian said calmly.

"What?" Holly said, trying to keep her voice calm as well.

"Being able to tell when people are lying to me," Adrian said. His yellow eyes seemed to bore into hers. "Out with it. What is happening? Where'd you really get the rose?"

Holly forgot about being panicked and got annoyed again by Adrian's stare. She wasn't going to be intimidated by Ol' Witchy-Eyes! It was perhaps for this reason that she overcompensated by blurting an answer that dared him not to believe it:

"I got it from a ghost gardener who was whispering in your ear while you checked for bugs on the root of that plant. He called it a 'Wildeve.' And he's standing right behind you."

Adrian looked—and saw nothing.

"The young master and I have an amicable relationship, miss," said the gardener, apparently amused by this. "He can't see me, but he does listen well. You see how well he's done with the garden—between his books and a little whispered advice now and then."

"He can hear you?" Holly was puzzled.

"I can hear what?" Adrian said, looking in the direction Holly was looking, bewildered.

"Some folks what are sensitive to it can hear us like whispers on the wind, miss," said the gardener. "Belike as he thinks what I say is his own idea, come to him as an inspiration, like."

"Oh." Holly said in a small voice.

Adrian was looking at her, but she couldn't interpret the look on his face; she had seen people look at her like she was crazy, knew the look of people who thought she was making it all up for attention, or the looks of people who were actually afraid of her. This was none of those.

Adrian appeared suspicious, but excited. He asked her outright: "Can you talk to ghosts?"

Holly, partly in shock now that this was all happening (and with the ghost watching the whole thing with a big grin on his face, all very well for him), simply replied:

"Yes."

"Do your parents know?" Adrian questioned further.

"Sort of? They don't believe me so I don't talk about it any more." Her face fell a little, sad memories playing across it.

Adrian took her hand. "I won't tell anyone, I promise," he said.

This was unexpected! It was Holly who now looked at Adrian in disbelief. "Really?" she said.

"I promise," he repeated. "I can't imagine how hard it is to keep that a secret. I'm guessing you didn't know the gardener was a ghost or you wouldn't have spoken to him?"

Holly nodded. "They—ghosts I mean—just look like people to me."

"What's his name? The gardener," Adrian said, squeezing her hand.

"It's just Tom, young master," grinned Tom.

Holly repeated this.

"Has he been helping me with the garden? Because it's really looking good and I knew it couldn't just be me and I thought Mum had hired someone—" Adrian seemed more and more excited by the idea.

"He has," Holly said. "He gives you hints, I think, and part of you can hear him but he says it probably just seems like inspiration or your own idea."

Adrian flung his arms out and spun around in place. "Thank you, Tom!" he said, his face aglow with the flush of discovery.

"You're most welcome, young master," Tom said, touching his cap again, and vanished.

"He—he said you're welcome and vanished. They do that," Holly stammered, at a loss for anything else to say. "Come and go, I mean."

Adrian looked her squarely in the eyes. This time, instead of his predatory stare, his eyes practically glowed with excitement. "Holly Weaver," he said. "You are the coolest person I have ever met."

Holly needed to sit down. She'd just accidentally outed herself to someone who not only believed her, but was excited by it all; it was a lot to take in. She moved towards one of the stone benches and sat, still in a bit of shock.

Adrian peppered her with questions: How long had she been able to see ghosts? Did they always give her things? Were there any scary ones?

She answered him as best she could—all her life, not always, and yes indeed there were—and found that talking about it, though new to her, felt wonderful, like putting down a heavy weight one hadn't realised one was carrying.

"They're only scary until you figure out what they want," she said. "Sometimes they don't know how to tell you and the scary parts are them trying to just get your attention. Some of them are really lonely, but mostly they're just people."

"But seriously though," she continued. "You really *can't* tell anyone. I'm worried I'll get locked in a loony bin or something."

Oddly, Adrian was smiling. "Oh, you don't have to worry. They'd have to lock me up too," he said.

"What do you mean?" Holly asked.

"It must run in families or something…" Adrian said more to himself than her.

"What does?" Holly said. She was getting suspicious. Adrian was acting strangely—at least compared to the last couple of hours she'd known him for.

"I showed you my secret garden. Now, do you want to see a *real* secret?"

"*Yes,*" Holly said, wishing Adrian would just get on and reveal whatever was going on in his head.

Adrian pointed at the little statue of the man riding a unicorn.

"Yeah, what about it?" Holly said.

"Giddy-up," Adrian said. And then the statue rose off the ground, and floated over to land beside the bench on which Holly was sitting.

Holly had been half-expecting Adrian to say—well, *anything*, but this was definitely not something she would have imagined.

"Did you... did you do that?" She asked, though she felt it was obviously unnecessary.

"I can move things with my mind," Adrian confirmed, excited now. "It only just started. I didn't know what was going on! But you... you're special too!"

"I don't feel very special," Holly said dourly, still trying to process the moment.

"Holly, don't you get it? We're...we're *magic*," Adrian said.

"I'm sure my parents would say something scientific," Holly said. *"Mutant aberrations* or *evolutionary offshoots* or something weird like that."

"Science schmience!" Adrian declared. "We're magic, you and me, special *proper* magic, and this is now going to be the best summer ever!"

As if to give the lie to his statement, the rain continued to fall from the rolling clouds of the grey sky.

Holly looked at her cousin and wondered if he might not be just a little bit crazy, himself, and asked herself if perhaps that was a good thing?

Just then they both heard their names being called, as well as a bell being rung (*"A dinner bell?"* thought Holly. *"Seriously?"*), and they had to halt their conversation.

"Come on, it's dinner time!" Adrian said as he reached for her hand.

Holly took it. "All right then," she said. Her cousin seemed aglow, as if he were on fire within; she had never been excited about what she could do, and now she'd met someone who could do what he'd done and perhaps it wasn't her, or him: perhaps it was *the world* that was crazy.

Deciding that to be the most probable case, she accompanied him as they left the garden.

Chapter 5: The Missing Boy

*"I do have a sense, and I've never not had
it, of how easily things can vanish."*
—Doris Lessing

The next day, Adrian's father left to go on a business trip ("I don't see why he has to actually travel," said Adrian to Holly, "I mean, haven't bankers ever heard of the Internet?") and Holly's parents were "popping down to London" for a science conference they had conveniently forgotten to tell Holly about ("Oh that's okay, Mom and Dad, don't bother staying here for more than five minutes, just drop me off like a load of laundry, it's fine!") which left them with Adrian's mother, Emily.

She, too, had plans to go out that day but unlike the other adults, her plans included the two cousins. She wanted to visit a gallery that was interested in her photographs ("Because she probably donated money to them," Adrian whispered to Holly) and afterwards wanted to take them to lunch and do a bit of sight-seeing.

Adrian beamed. "This is going to be great!" he said. "I seriously thought we were going to just be, you know, abandoned all summer. But look! It's like we actually exist!" he grinned.

Holly smiled at his enthusiasm but couldn't help but feel a little bit sad that Adrian assumed he'd be abandoned by his parents. She sympathised—her parents could really get their heads buried in their work and forget to come up for air—meaning sometimes it seemed like they forgot they had a daughter. But she'd never thought of it as abandonment. Perhaps Adrian's view was different because he spent all year at boarding school and only got to spend summer and Christmas at home?

Ugh. If that's the case, she thought, *I bet he's lonely all the time.*

Well, if she and Adrian were in the same boat, she thought, then at least they were in it together.

Aunt Emily swept into the room, wearing a tiny, neat jacket and donning what Holly assumed were driving gloves. "Are we ready, dears?" she chirped.

————

As they drove through town, Holly observed that Colchester was a neat place, with equal parts old-world charm right next to modern, like English pubs with names like *The Slug and Lettuce* or *The Three Wise Monkeys* being next door to Taco Bell. She was pleased to see American franchises were as available in England as they were in Boston; it made her feel more at home.

Aunt Emily had parked the car and told them they could wander up and down the high street, but to be back at the gallery in an hour, so she and Adrian were taking advantage of the time to do a little sight-seeing of their own.

Adrian, for his part, noticed Holly had become quiet, withdrawn; she stayed close to him and appeared to be staring mostly at the ground. The change was so rapid that he asked her what was wrong.

"It's a new town," she said as if that explained everything.

"Well yes," Adrian said gently, "but there are lots of things to see, and I'm with you, you won't need to worry about getting lost—"

"It's not that," Holly said and now she looked into his eyes, and he could see her nervousness blinking out from hers. "It's—when I'm in a new place, with new people, especially a big place like downtown on the High Street or whatever you call it, I'm never sure..."

"Never sure about what?" he said, looking around as if for some kind of threat.

"Never sure who's *real*, and who's..." she let her words trail off.

Adrian took her hand. "Oh," he said with sympathy. What must it be like for his cousin, he wondered, never knowing who was a living person and who was a ghost? He supposed that to others, she might just appear to be talking to thin air, looking mad as a hatter while having no idea at all that she was doing it.

"Well, you stick by me. I'll be your guide and interpreter on your tour of Colchester's High Street," he said cheerily. "I'll squeeze your hand if I can see a person who talks to you, that way you'll know they're not a ghost."

Holly blushed and nodded. "That sounds okay." But she still appeared nervous.

Adrian paused. "You know what we need?" he said.

Holly looked at him. "What?"

"Jacket potatoes."

"What are those?"

"There," he said, pointing to a bright red truck parked on the side of the street, where people were lined up. "Come on."

He led her over to the truck, which was a street-food vending truck, which had a big sign on the side which clearly advertised "Duke's Jacket Potatoes."

As it turned out, "jacket potatoes" were just baked potatoes, served with a variety of condiments like butter, chives, cheese, even meat like tuna. Holly read the sign and saw that you could order a potato any way you liked it, and they even gave you a little fork and knife to eat it with.

Adrian had his with some kind of brown sauce and bacon, and she chose cheese and chives, and Adrian paid for them. "My treat," he said, "Welcome to England, home of the jacket potato."

Holly laughed, and suddenly, to Adrian, her mood seemed to break as they sat on a nearby little bench to enjoy their treat, and Holly began to tell him a bit about Boston and the similarities to Colchester.

Adrian smiled and felt as if the day had gotten better, and they could now concentrate on having a nice time.

As it turned out, he was wrong.

———

Adrian's mother was waiting for them as they returned to the photo gallery. She was on her phone, and her voice was anxious.

She hung up the phone, her face a mask of worry.

"What's wrong, Mum?" asked Adrian.

"I'm sorry dears, we shall have to postpone lunch. That was my friend, Mrs. Clarke. Her son Ethan has gone missing."

Mrs. Whitingham bundled the cousins into the back seat of her car.

"What do you mean he's missing, Mum?" asked Adrian.

"Well dear, I'm sure you didn't know this, but the Clarkes had just put their house up for sale. This morning, poor Lydia—that's Mrs. Clarke to you—went up to wake Ethan and found his bed empty. She's looked for him all morning and found nothing; she's beside herself."

"Has she telephoned the police?" asked Adrian, frowning in thought.

"What a question, Adrian! Of course she has!" his mother said with some asperity.

Adrian seemed to consider this. Holly noticed the "deep-thought" lines as he furrowed his brow and wondered what was going on in his head.

"And we're going to visit her, Mum? To console her?" Adrian put his hand to his chin, as if mulling this over.

"Well yes, that's why I'm driving over there straight away. Do you two think you can stay out of trouble while I comfort poor Lydia?"

"Not at all," said Adrian, with a secret grin. But his mother was concentrating on her driving, and had stopped listening.

—————

During the ride over to the Clarkes', Holly wondered what it was that Adrian was up to. Most people would react to the news of a missing boy with shock, or surprise—but it seemed Adrian had gone into a kind of quiet heavy-thinking mode that she didn't understand.

She was uncomfortable, to say the least. Mrs. Whitingham was concentrating and wasn't speaking, Adrian was in his own head and if she was being honest, kind of freaking her out a little. She felt isolated and alone, and didn't trust this new situation.

Summer vacation had, it seemed, taken a left turn at the village of Weird and was heading straight toward the town of No Thank You as far as she was concerned.

She tried to engage her cousin in conversation. "I'm sorry about your friend," she said.

"Oh, we weren't friends. We only ever met once, I think." Adrian said matter-of-factly.

Holly's brow furrowed. "But he was your neighbour... well, sort of. You must have played together loads of times."

Adrian shook his head. "No. I've never really...um... played with anybody."

Surprised, she looked at him. "You must be very lonely," she said simply.

"Not really," Adrian replied. "I find myself to be excellent company." And he flashed her a grin that Holly didn't quite believe.

After an uncomfortably long silence, they pulled into the driveway of a pretty country home, a two-story affair much more like a real house and not the massive mansion that was Locksley Hall.

At the front door, Adrian's mother rang the bell and the door opened to reveal a dishevelled-looking woman whose curly hair hung this way and that, framing a face that was puffy from crying.

"Lydia!" said Mrs. Whitingham.

"Oh, Emily," sobbed Mrs. Clarke as they embraced. Adrian and Holly stood awkwardly for a moment before Adrian's mother remembered to introduce them.

"Oh—I'm sorry, Lydia. You remember my son, Adrian? And this is his cousin, Holly Weaver."

"Of course," said Mrs. Clarke. "And how d'you do, dear," she said, shaking Holly's hand. Holly gave her a polite "Fine, thank you." What could she say to someone whose son was missing?

Adrian piped up: "Can we see Ethan's room?"

His mother turned to him with a shocked expression. "Whatever for?" she said.

Adrian answered: "A kid's room is their whole world. It's their personality. It's their everything. If there are clues to Ethan's whereabouts, they'll be in there."

Mrs. Whitingham added "looking rather cross" to her shocked expression and opened her mouth to speak, when a desperate-looking Mrs. Clarke interrupted her.

"And what makes you think you can discover such clues?" she asked, searching Adrian's face.

"I've been told I'm very observant," said Adrian—and he looked so serious that it seemed to convince Mrs. Clarke.

She sighed and put her hand on Mrs. Whitingham's shoulder. "Oh let him, Emily. It'll give them something to do." she said.

"Thank you, Mrs. Clarke," said Adrian with such solemn courtesy it made him sound like a miniature adult.

"Upstairs, second door on the right," she said, and pointed. Holly and Adrian headed upstairs.

Once they were upstairs and the two women downstairs were out of earshot, Holly said to Adrian: "What do you think you're doing?"

Adrian said, as if it were the most obvious thing in the world, "I'm going to look for clues relating to Ethan's disappearance, of course."

"Why?" Holly asked, bluntly.

"Why? To help, of course. Didn't you see his mum? She's beside herself. Don't you want to help her?"

"Well of course, but we're not the police, Adrian." Holly said.

"No, we're better. We're *magic*," Adrian said.

"We're what?" Holly said, guardedly.

"You know. Magic. We can look for clues that other people can't find. You can talk to ghosts and ask them things, and I—"

Holly stopped outside the bedroom door. "It doesn't work like that," she said flatly.

Adrian's brow furrowed in puzzlement. "It doesn't?"

"*No,*" Holly said in frustration. "I can't *summon* ghosts. I don't *call* them. They just—they just show up on their own. And like I said, some of them aren't so nice."

This only seemed to excite Adrian. "But just imagine all the information they'd have—"

Holly put up a hand to stop him, and now she looked a bit angry.

"Of course *you're* excited. *Your* magic doesn't show up at the foot of your bed at two in the morning shrieking or moaning. *Your* magic doesn't follow you to school and keep acting out how it died while you're trying to concentrate on your math lesson. *Your* magic is something you can choose when and how to use. You can choose *not* to use it. Some of us don't get that luxury."

And here she paused, and looked furious. Adrian saw the look and immediately apologised.

"I'm sorry. It just didn't occur to me." He said, tentatively squeezing her arm.

"I'm sorry too. I don't mean to be so angry about it, but when I stop and think about it all, it can be overwhelming. It really can be too much, sometimes."

"Do you want to leave? Go outside or something?" Adrian appeared concerned.

"And miss out on these supposed clues you're so sure will be in there? Not likely." She said, managing a grin.

Adrian smiled. "You're a brave one," he said, and gave her a hug.

He looked at her with his impish eyes. "Do you want to solve a mystery?" he asked as he opened the door.

Ethan's room was uncharacteristically-for-a-boy tidy; Adrian mused aloud that it was probably because his family were selling the house.

Holly chimed in with: "That would explain the neatly-packed box labelled 'toys' that's in this closet," she said, stepping back from the closet door to reveal a large, taped-shut cardboard box with TOYS written on it in black marker.

Adrian nodded. "This creates a problem for us; the tidier the room, the harder it is to see if anything's missing."

"Why would something be missing?" Holly asked.

"Well, if Ethan had run away, for example, he might have brought a favourite toy or keepsake along with him. But his toys are packed away and this room is more like a display piece than a lived-in boy's room at the moment," Adrian said.

Holly said, "Mm. I see. There's a flaw with that logic, though. You said you didn't really know him. So how would you know if anything was missing? Also, you're looking for what's not here. I'm looking at what *is* here."

"Such as?" Adrian asked, annoyed that she was right.

"Well, I mean it's obvious there were no signs of a struggle—either in this room or somewhere else, or Mrs. Clarke would be a lot more agitated than she is. This room is still nice and neat. This also tells us that Ethan didn't, for example, have an angry tantrum in here, which implies that he wasn't angry about moving."

Adrian paused, then said "You really *are* clever, aren't you," his annoyance giving way to admiration.

"I am," said Holly. "What, girls can't be clever?" Her brow furrowed.

"Not that," Adrian said, holding up his hands. "It's just that all the people I know at school don't like to *think*. They just like things handed to them, you understand? They would just accept this situation, they wouldn't spend time trying to figure it out. But you just had a great insight and it's very cool, is all I meant to say."

Holly relaxed and even blushed a little. "Aw. It ain't nothin'," she said, which made Adrian wince.

"Must you murder the English language?" he complained.

"I do what I want," said Holly, which made Adrian laugh. "But back to this mystery. If we assume that Ethan didn't walk out of here on purpose, or get taken out of here against his will, what does that leave?"

Adrian pondered. "Would you know if he were dead?"

Holly gasped and smacked him on the arm. "Adrian, that is a horribly creepy thing to say. You don't just blurt out a question like that."

Adrian shrugged. "How am I supposed to ask it, then?"

Holly shook her head. "I'm more concerned that you don't get that it's creepy to casually ask if a boy our age has died, than I am with his actually possibly being dead."

Adrian's eyes widened. "*Now* who's being creepy?"

Holly looked back at him uncomprehendingly. "What?"

"Ugh. Never mind," Adrian said. "But can you tell if he's...if he's a ghost?"

"Ugh," Holly said, echoing him. "Fine. Give me a minute. Just stand there and be quiet, okay?"

Holly closed her eyes. She stood quite still, hearing at first only the sounds of her own breathing, and Adrian's.

She knew that sometimes ghosts whispered, even when they weren't "awake." It was like they were talking in their sleep sometimes, speaking old memories aloud in quiet voices only she could hear; when she was younger, in her bed at night, the sounds of the whispering dead had sometimes surrounded her and frightened her.

She had since learned that it was only the voices of people long since gone, talking about things of yesterday or long ago, of lost loves or old dreams or even (in one case) their shopping list.

That had made it easier on her, realising that ghost whispers were just people nattering on about what was important to them, things that they could no longer do or that they missed and wanted back. It was very sad sometimes, but it was also, she had decided, like a kind of love—repeating to yourself over and over again a list of things you cared about. She liked that better, and it had helped her get over a lot of her early fears about the ghosts she heard.

Not that all ghosts were tragic, lovely figures—not at all. Some of them were angry, still angry over whatever wrong had been done to them, seeking revenge and looking for any way to make it happen…

She shook her head slightly to clear that thought. That was definitely not the sort of thing she should be concentrating on at this particular moment. No, it was time to listen to the present, not the past, but the here and now.

She felt someone or something watching her. It wasn't Adrian. In her otherworldly sense he was like the background of a stage, like the inanimate furniture, alive but not relevant to whatever part of her brain that was attempting to communicate with the ghost world.

There was some kind of—of *feeling*—but it wasn't like a whisper, or any kind of voice that she could hear with her ears. It was more of an echo, a sense of something that had been said before when she wasn't in the room, the vibrations of which still hung in the air when she entered.

"Don't."

A faint kind of feeling of loss, or rather trying to prevent loss.

"Don't."

Don't what?

"Don't leave."

Ah! Holly realised the feeling of loss was like the feeling of missing someone—someone who was leaving but who had not yet gone. She felt it all around her, as if many voices were saying the same thing at the same time, but quietly and intensely instead of shouting loudly.

"DON'T LEAVE ME."

An overwhelming sadness suddenly poured forth, a feeling of incredible loneliness, the sense of being left all alone, left behind and forgotten, like a child's favourite toy misplaced under the bed, like a beloved pet who had run away and gotten lost.

Holly opened her eyes with a gasp and immediately began sobbing. "Oh," she said, "It's so *sad!* Missing. Longing, mourning. Oh don't. Don't leave me! Don't leave me alone!" she said between hiccupping sobs.

Adrian was by her side immediately. "Holly? What's wrong? What happened? Come back to me, look at me!" He gently put his hands on her shoulders. "It's me, Adrian, see? I'm here! I'm not leaving. I'm right here. It's okay. It's really okay!"

Through her tears she could see Adrian's concerned face, his yellow eyes searching hers, trying to figure out how he could help. This brought her back to now, the real non-whispery *now*, and she threw her arms around him.

"I'm fine, I'm okay, I'm fine," she repeated in a way that didn't exactly reassure Adrian that it was true. She took a deep breath and composed herself, wiping the tears from her eyes.

"Okay, wow, that was intense," she said, sniffling a bit as she began to feel more normal.

"What happened?" Adrian said. "Was there a ghost?"

Holly almost laughed at the question. "No. There was just a strong feeling. A feeling of missing someone, of being left behind, a lonely feeling like being abandoned by someone you love."

Adrian's face crinkled up in a frown. "That's horrible. That's very sad."

"Tell me about it," Holly said. "But it wasn't like a ghost. They whisper sometimes, or speak to me directly, right to my face. This wasn't like that *at all*. It was like walking into a room where someone's been crying and even though you weren't there when they were, you can tell that the room is just sad. You know?"

"I think so," Adrian replied. "I've walked into the room after my parents have had an argument and I can tell that they have had. Like there's an echo of it left over."

"Exactly!" Holly said. "This is like that. But the weird thing is, I've never experienced this before. I didn't see the ghost, I didn't even really hear it—I just kind of *felt* it. Like it had been and gone."

Adrian frowned. "So if, perhaps, Ethan had died—"

"Will you stop talking about Ethan as if he's dead? It's just so creepy! Seriously, Adrian!" Holly exclaimed.

"But how are we to solve his disappearance unless we know if he is or isn't?" Adrian replied as if the discussion were a matter of course.

"Adrian." said Holly, and now it was her turn to place her hands on his shoulders, as if to steady him and make him pay attention to her: "I can't tell if someone has become a ghost. Sometimes not even if they're standing right in front of me, remember? It's not like there's a bell that rings every time someone pops off to the Other Side or whatever," she said, exasperated. "Please stop treating this thing I have like it's some great game you want to play."

Adrian looked hurt. "I only wanted to help find Ethan," he said sadly.

"I know, but look—all I can tell you is that this is a very sad room to be in and that he is not in it, ghost or no ghost. Okay?"

"Okay," Adrian agreed. He looked listlessly around the too-clean room. "If only we knew who his friends were, we could ask if they've seen him—"

Holly interrupted: "That is the kind of thing the police do. That I'm sure they are doing, right now."

Adrian nodded, pondering for a moment.

Then his head snapped up. "Wait. There *are* people we can ask if they've seen Ethan, that the police can't ask!"

Holly cocked her head to the side. "Who would that be?" she asked.

Adrian grinned his mad, Cheshire Cat grin to indicate that he'd had a truly grand idea.

"Do you remember when we drove up—there's a little country graveyard just down the lane."

Holly understood his intent instantly. "No. Absolutely not. No way," she said.

Adrian took her hand and held it in both his own. "I know that you have just had a very sad experience," he said solemnly. "But Holly, you're the only person that can do this. Your gift—your special magic—could help find a missing boy. You'd be saving him, and saving his parents a ton of worry. You'd be a hero."

Holly sighed. Adrian had a way with words; she couldn't help but be a little bit convinced by them. *I must be nuts to even consider this,* she thought.

"Okay." She said.

"Yay!" Adrian jumped for joy.

Yep. Definitely nuts, she thought.

Chapter 6: The Graveyard Gathering

"Cemeteries used to be nice and quiet.
Now they're teeming with life."

—Anthony T. Hincks

The little village graveyard was, as it happened, an easy walking distance down the lane. Adrian had asked his mother if he and Holly could go for a walk and his mother, apparently relieved to have them outside while she comforted her friend, thought it was a splendid idea.

As they strolled, Adrian asked: "So… I'm guessing by your reaction that cemeteries are usually a bad idea for you?"

Holly snorted. "Picture walking into a room. There's a party going on, but you haven't been invited. And as you walk in, everyone turns to look at you because you're new and interesting, or because they see you as a trespasser or intruder. And then they all start to move toward you, like a big wave of people, because they're curious or because they're angry that you've interrupted them or because they are so unbelievably lonely and desperate for living warmth that they want to reach out and embrace you...all at once."

Adrian paused. "Wow." He said quietly. "Now I feel like a real thicko for suggesting this."

Holly wrinkled her nose. "What's a thicko?"

Adrian laughed a small, quiet laugh. "It means thick-headed. When someone is thick it's hard to get ideas through to them. They're a thicko."

"You're not a thicko. You just don't know what it's like, is all. There's no shame in being ignorant of a thing if you don't have all the facts," Holly said.

"Thank you. But now that you've told me what it's like...maybe we shouldn't go to the cemetery. It sounds like it could be overwhelming."

"Believe it or not, it's actually easier during the day. I don't know why but most ghosts are night people," she grinned.

Adrian seemed doubtful. "Well, if you're sure," he said.

Truthfully, Holly wasn't sure—but she had said she would do it and if there was one thing Holly believed in, it was doing what she said she would.

When they arrived at the little chapel that opened on to the cemetery, Holly was pleased to see that it was a small village graveyard and not some giant only-one-in-the-whole-city necropolis (a cool word that she had read that meant "city of the dead"). No, this was… *quaint,* she thought.

She saw a few people wandering among the gravestones, but not many. They could perhaps have been family members visiting, but their clothes seemed haphazard and perhaps out of date.

Holly silently cursed the current fashion trend of mixing and matching things from previous years, even decades, with current clothes; it made it really hard to pick out if someone was a ghost based on how they dressed.

Fortunately, she had Adrian with her. He had promised to help her with exactly this sort of thing. "Do you see any people in the graveyard?" she asked him.

He took her hand. "No," he said. "Do you?"

"Yup," she said. "Milling about. Maybe four or five. Like they're having a lovely afternoon stroll."

"Should we—" Adrian began, then checked himself. "Do you feel like trying to talk to them?"

Holly looked around; the day was sunny in parts, and there were patches of dappled sunlight on the ground that made the cemetery seem more earthly and less ghostly. She looked over at the line of small trees which shaded part of the area and said, "I'd like to stay in the sunshine if we could. It makes things less creepy."

"Understood," Adrian said, and squeezed her hand.

Holly led him over to a sunlit gravestone whose inscribed name had long since worn away; though she knew Adrian couldn't see her, there was a lady there in a nice floral dress with a brooch on it; she was older but still seemed spry, like a young grandmother who was still energetic. She had a kind face, and seemed more interested in picking weeds from around the gravestone—tidying up the place, apparently—than she was in the two children.

Holly cleared her throat politely. "Um, excuse me?" she said.

The lady turned. "Oh, my dear, you gave me a fright," she said, her hand touching the pearl necklace she wore.

"I...um...I'm looking for a friend of mine," Holly said. "His name is Ethan. He lives just up the road there," she said and she pointed toward the Clarke residence.

"Oh my dear, I'm afraid I'm not of much use," said the lady. "I tend to keep my attention on my own little patch, here. I—" she paused. "Did you say, 'lives' up the road? Present tense?"

Holly felt a cold prickly sensation on the back of her neck. "I...yes," she said, unsure what else to say.

"Dear, are you...how shall I put it… among the living?" the lady said, seeming quite surprised.

"I am," Holly said, squeezing Adrian's hand for comfort. Adrian was looking around blankly, as if trying to see, but unable to do so.

"Bless me, I've never met one of you before. Oh, excuse me, how rude! I simply mean a living one that can see those of us who've passed on. How rare and wonderful! I'm Mrs. Littlewood, dear, Kate Littlewood. That's me over there," she said, pointing to a grave which Holly saw bore her name.

"What's happening?" Adrian said, getting antsy from only hearing half the conversation.

"I met a lady named Mrs. Littlewood, we're making introductions," Holly told him.

"Who are you talking to, dear?" asked Mrs. Littlewood.

Just as most people couldn't see or hear ghosts, so too was it common for ghosts to not be able to see the living except when the time or place was just right. Holly had figured this out when several ghosts had walked right through her without noticing her. It had been unpleasant; ghosts were cold and they made your hair stand up and made you feel chilly when they walked through you.

"Oh, just my cousin," Holly replied politely.

"Oh, is he nearby—oh goodness, there he is. Yes, yes I see him now. Bless him, blending right into the background, isn't he! But yes, what a handsome young man!"

Adrian, of course, did not respond.

"Oh. Is he...not like you, dear?"

Holly shook her head. "No. He's special in other ways," she said.

"Oi," said Adrian. "No fair talking about me behind my back in front of my face!" His eyebrows furrowed together in frustration.

Holly stifled a giggle. "Sorry," she said.

She once again addressed the ghost: "Forgive us, Mrs. Littlewood. We need to find out what happened to Ethan. I suppose we'll need to continue asking around."

The lady paused, stroking her chin in thought. "Just a moment..." she said. "I do know some others who are more...shall we say 'well-travelled' than I," she continued. "I could make some introductions and you could ask your questions of them. Would that be all right?"

Holly was comforted by this particular ghost's marvellous manners. "Yes please," she said.

"Very well. Come for tea and I'll introduce you around."

Holly stopped. "Tea?" she asked.

"Tea?" Adrian echoed, looking confused.

"Yes, my dears. Follow me, if you would!" and she set off across the graveyard, toward the trees.

"The ghost just invited us for tea," Holly said, trying to make sense of it.

"Is that a thing that happens often?" Adrian asked.

"No. I mean, I've had ghosts bring me tea but I've never been to a ghost tea party." Holly looked at Adrian with a shrug and an "I have no idea how this works" look on her face.

"Well then," said Adrian. "I suggest we accept her invitation."

Still holding hands, Holly taking the lead, they followed Mrs. Littlewood into the trees.

————

For Adrian, it was all a bit strange; he was standing in a quiet, simple graveyard, holding his cousin's hand, while she talked to the air.

He felt a pang of jealousy; it was so cool that she could see and talk to ghosts! But then, he corrected himself. He ought not to be jealous of Holly's magic given what she had told him of it. And too, he had his own magic and oughtn't he be satisfied with the gift he had?

He supposed it was all right to want more, to do more, to be more—so long as he remembered to appreciate what he had and not be greedy about it. He'd read stories where the boy was the hero and had all the nice things and the girls, if any there were, were more sort of afterthoughts.

Holly was brave, smart and cool—so yes, perhaps it was okay to be a little jealous of her. And to be fascinated by her. When he'd been told a cousin was coming to visit for the summer, he certainly hadn't anticipated having this much fun or having so much in common.

Then Holly was tugging on his hand. "Mrs. Littlewood says it's just through here," she said, pointing.

Adrian saw two trees that were oddly growing in opposite directions—one up and to the left, and the other up and to the right. If you walked toward them a certain way, like they were now doing, it looked as though the trees formed a kind of triangular arch.

No sooner had they walked through the arch than it was as if the sun had gone behind a cloud; the warm sunlight became a kind of cool grey light, and the air a little chillier than it had been, though not quite what one would call cold.

The small line of trees had now become a kind of forest; Adrian couldn't see through the dense growth and the graveyard had quite gone. He could still see the arch made by the two trees but looking through it, he could only see more trees.

Apprehension took him; what if they couldn't get back to where they were? And where exactly were they now? Certainly not in the real world, where there had been sun and where the trees were only a thin line one could easily see through.

He looked up; he saw only cloudy grey sky, though it was bright like a misty morning. He decided it wasn't scary here, only...*strange*, was the only word he could think of.

Holly was still tugging him forward when he realised he could see who was leading her: Mrs. Littlewood, he presumed, as he could now see the lady in the floral dress and pearl necklace. To his surprise, she was neither transparent nor decayed-looking as he assumed ghosts must look; she was a person, a *whole* person, and as far as he could tell there was nothing ghostlike about her at all.

He was about to exclaim that he could see her when suddenly they seemed to turn, as if they had been walking in one direction and then changed, though Adrian never felt his feet leave the ground. They were just simply *there*, and "there" was a most curious sight, indeed.

There was a clearing, and all the trees that surrounded it were festooned with trinkets, jewellery, fairy lights, and shinies from bygone ages. A silver locket here, a brass doorknob there, a dozen little mirrors hanging in the branches all around; necklaces and string and little crystals on fishing lines; the whole effect was that of some mad ballroom, as if instead of a proper chandelier, those that had made it had just put together everything they could that reminded them of what a chandelier was, and had strung the bits and bobs all throughout the trees.

Adrian had a moment where he wondered where the electricity powering the Christmasy fairy lights was coming from, but his attention was distracted by the large dining table that served as the centrepiece of the odd clearing.

His first thought was that he'd found himself at the Mad Hatter's tea party, as all the chairs around the table were of different shapes and sizes from modern to years gone by. They all looked well-worn and comfortable; high-backed wooden chairs and overstuffed lounge chairs and tall stools and ones that looked to be straight from a common kitchen set.

On the table itself was the most motley assortment of delicious-looking things; muffins and iced cakes and toast and butter and cream, jars of jam, little finger sandwiches and tureens of soup and everything that made a proper tea, plus a little bit of lunch as well: meats and cheeses and little dishes of pickles and other fixings.

The plates and cutlery were, like the chairs, a hodgepodge of styles and designs; few things matched and they seemed to be from all over the world; German and English china plates with American silverware and French soup bowls; and a lovely woven tablecloth that looked as if it were from India.

"Wow," he finally managed.

Holly turned to him. "You can see this?"

Adrian replied: "If by 'this' you mean this fantastical tea party forest ballroom, yes, and Mrs. Littlewood, too. Hello, ma'am," he said, waving to her.

"Ah, there you are," said Mrs. Littlewood with delight. "You're much clearer now."

"How come he can see you now?" Holly asked.

"Well," said Mrs. Littlewood, "You're in our place now, dear. The spirit world. Sort of *chez nous*, as the French say. Since we're both here, we have a sort of...I guess you'd call it *equality*."

Adrian whistled. "We're in the ghost world," he said.

"Not quite, dear," Mrs. Littlewood corrected him. "I did say *spirit* world. There are more spirits than just the ghosts of the dearly departed, as it happens."

It was Holly's turn to look astonished. "What do you mean, 'more than just ghosts?'"

Mrs. Littlewood smiled. "Everything has a spirit, dear. Trees, birds, even some automobiles. Haven't you ever noticed that things can take on a sort of mood or personality over time? That's its spirit. This is the world where all of those spirits are from and to where they return when their time in the living world is done. It's all quite neighbourly, really, when you think about it—like going out to visit someone and then returning home."

Holly's mind was buzzing with questions. "But then how... why do they... what..." she stammered, all the questions trying to push through to be asked first.

"Questions later, dear," she said. "Let me introduce you around."

A smiling East Indian man was approaching them. Adrian thought perhaps his suit was from just a few years ago. He did not look very old; perhaps the same age as Adrian's father? It was difficult to tell.

"This is Mr. Chakravarty," Mrs. Littlewood said. "Never fear, we're all quite a friendly bunch. Isn't that so, Mr. C?"

"Most assuredly," grinned the man as he sketched a small bow in the direction of Adrian and Holly.

"And here comes Miss Plumb," she said, as a young lady with wavy hair (looking very much like a soda ad from the 1920s) smiled and offered a hand to Adrian in greeting. Adrian shook it; it was cool but not cold, another thing he had not expected of a ghost.

"Charmed! Abso*lute*ly charmed!" Miss Plumb said vigorously. "How lovely to make new acquaintances. Evelyn Plumb. Goodness, you do look alike. Are you brother and sister?"

"Cousins," said Adrian.

Miss Plumb shook her head appreciatively. "Marvelous. Truly marvelous. The family resemblance is uncanny."

"Thank you," said Holly.

"Oi, you lot. What's all the palaver?" said a boy not much older than Adrian, wearing knee-length breeches, a homespun white shirt and leather vest. Adrian noted that he was also barefoot, his dirty feet appearing as if they had not seen the inside of a shoe in years.

"What's 'palaver?'" asked Holly.

"It's like 'blabber,'" Adrian said. "Or 'hullabaloo.' It basically means a confusing amount of conversation, or just noise."

"Puh-LA-ver," giggled Holly. "Noted. Good word, um...?" she said, looking at the boy.

"Matthew, miss," he said, tugging on a forelock of his hair as if touching the brim of a cap. "And I surely didn't mean anything as disrespectful as all that," he said, looking at Adrian reproachfully, who shrugged.

"So what brings you to our woods?" Matthew asked.

Adrian felt an odd little pang of jealousy at the way Matthew looked at Holly—as if she fascinated him. Which of course she probably did, but after all he had been fascinated first! He swallowed and had to mentally tell himself to relax.

Mrs. Littlewood spoke up. "These two lovely young people are looking for a friend of theirs, Matthew," she said.

"Oh, aye?" Matthew responded, apparently having not noticed Adrian's sudden tension. "There's lots of new ones always looking for their friends, and that's the way of it, I guess. But come, we're about to tuck in!"

"Tuck in?" asked Holly.

"Oh yes dear," said Mrs. Littlewood. "I wasn't joking about tea. Although luncheon would perhaps be a more apt description."

"Looks like we're lunching today after all," said Adrian. Holly rolled her eyes. *Boys and food. Feed a boy and he'll accept anything,* she thought.

"Come dears, you can sit by me," Mrs. Littlewood said as she ushered them toward the splendidly eclectic table before them.

She escorted them to seats near the end, while Matthew, Miss Plumb, and Mr. Chakravarty all selected chairs up the length of the table.

Holly noticed a rather grand chair at the head of the table remained empty. She whispered to Mrs. Littlewood: "Whose chair is that?"

"Ah," said the lady as she delicately placed her napkin on her lap. "That would be Lady Arngrim's."

"Who—" Holly began, but Mrs. Littlewood continued: "Lady Arngrim is the oldest of our little band. She's a trifle old-fashioned; I should perhaps caution you to be on your best behaviour around her. Do not speak out of turn—in fact, best you don't speak at all unless addressed—and always remember your manners, and you'll be fine."

Holly frowned. To her, Lady Arngrim sounded like some kind of unpleasant grandparent that was all rules and no fun.

"But where is she?" Holly asked.

Just then, a soft moan was heard as a wind seemed to rush through the trees, though they remained perfectly still. The lights, however, began to flicker on and off in random patterns, and the tiny ornaments in the trees began to jingle and jangle as if they were being shaken by unseen hands. Thunder rumbled in the distance.

"What is going on?" asked Adrian, looking around at the chaos that was happening around, but not to, the table.

"Lady Arngrim does like to make an entrance, dear. Just be patient." answered Mrs. Littlewood.

Just then, a flash of lightning overhead followed by a loud clap of thunder nearly jolted Holly and Adrian right out of their seats, gasping in shock as, suddenly, a regal figure appeared at the head of the table.

She was an older woman, but it was hard to tell how old exactly; she wore a powdered white wig all done up in curls, pale face make-up smoothing out any lines that might have shown her true age.

She wore an incredibly elaborate gown of silk and brocade, hand-sewn pearls adorning the bodice. Her hands were clad in silk gloves, and she was fanning herself with an ornate fan.

"Lady Arngrim, I presume?" whispered Adrian.

"Shh," said Matthew from across the table, glancing nervously at Lady Arngrim, who seemed not to have noticed. Adrian frowned.

"Good afternoon, everyone," she said. She had a light voice, but there was iron in it—this was a powerful woman. Holly thought she seemed quite used to being the centre of attention.

"Good afternoon, Your Ladyship," said the other four. Holly and Adrian, not sure what the proper etiquette was, stayed silent.

"I trust you are all well? Ah! Of course I mean, 'as well as can be expected,' don't I?" and she chuckled gracefully.

The four ghosts laughed appreciatively. To Adrian and Holly, it sounded forced and insincere.

She sat in the head chair, and opened her fan. "Oh! I see there are two new faces at our table. Who will make introductions?"

Mrs. Littlewood stood up. "I shall, if it pleases your Ladyship," she said politely.

"It does, my dear, it does indeed. Proceed," said Lady Arngrim regally.

Holly decided she couldn't stand the woman. She had only seen her for a minute or two but she was so full of herself, Holly could scarcely believe it. She glanced at Adrian, whose eyes were glued to Lady Arngrim but, rather than being cowed by her grandeur, seemed to be looking at her in a more calculated fashion. Holly thought by the expression on his face that Adrian didn't trust her and was being cautious and wary.

Kind of like how he looked at me when we first met, she realised.

"May I present…er…? Dears, what are your names and where are you from?" She turned to them both with a questioning expression.

"Holly Weaver of Boston, USA," said Holly.

"Adrian Whitingham of Locksley Hall, Colchester, England," said Adrian.

"Adrian and Holly," Mrs. Littlewood said with a flourish. Though rather unnecessarily, Holly thought, since both she and Adrian had answered for themselves.

Lady Arngrim seemed to take this in stride. "I see by your clothes you are very modern. Newly among us, I presume?" She asked, lightly fanning herself.

"Er…we only just arrived," said Holly.

"Yes, yes, I could tell the instant I saw you. Poor dears. I greet you and bid you welcome to this table. Welcome, welcome," she said, gesturing with her fan.

"But my goodness, where are my manners?" smiled the Lady as she picked up a small silver bell that had been beside her plate. "Do let us begin." She rang the bell, a beautiful silvery kind of sound coming from it as she closed her eyes, listening to it.

"Hands, please," she said.

Everyone else was joining hands; Mrs. Littlewood took Holly's hand and Mr. Chakravarty took Adrian's. There was a kind of hum around the table; not the sort you could actually hear but more the sort that you felt, as if a current of electricity were passing from person to person.

Lady Arngrim closed her eyes, and spoke in a rhythmic, melodic voice:

"Bless this table and all who sit;

This fellowship of kindred spirits,

Bless all those who've gone before,

For this day and ever more."

Adrian shivered. There was something in Lady Arngrim's voice that made him feel cold; as if she were speaking from a faraway place he couldn't see, but from which her voice could still be heard. It was creepy!

"Shall we begin?" said Lady Arngrim brightly, as she began to help herself to the delicacies before her; the others began to follow suit.

Holly put a hand on Adrian's arm as he reached for a platter. "Don't," she said.

Adrian frowned, clearly tempted by the sight of the food. "Whyever not?" he asked.

"I read a story a while ago. I can't remember all of it but there was a man who had a meal with a friend who had long since died and become a ghost. And because the man ate with him, he became a ghost himself. One of the lines from the story was 'He who dines with a dead man, himself becomes a dead man'."

Adrian looked with suspicion at the table. "It seems fine to me."

"Had a lot of experience with ghost food, have you?" Holly said.

"You said before that ghosts had brought you tea," Adrian said accusingly.

"Yes, they brought me tea from the real world," Holly said with exasperation. "They didn't bring me *ghost* tea." But then she realised: she had no way of knowing where the tea had come from. Perhaps it had been ghost tea, after all? She shivered at the thought.

Adrian saw the perplexed look on her face. "You're not so sure, are you?" he said.

"My dears, whatever are you arguing about?" Mrs. Littlewood interrupted. She cast nervous glances toward Lady Arngrim, but Mr. Chakravarty seemed to be holding her attention with conversation.

"Holly doesn't think we should eat ghost food because then we'll be ghosts," Adrian blurted out. Holly kicked him under the table. "Ow!" he exclaimed.

Mrs. Littlewood laughed gently. "Oh my dear, you are very clever to be so thoughtful. But perhaps you don't quite understand what this is? What you are seeing is not so much 'ghost food,' as you put it, but rather the memories we all have of nice meals we've had."

"What?" Holly asked, confused.

"We feast not on food but on memories, dear, and the table is always full. Sunday lunches and Christmas feasts and warm, cozy Tuesday evenings where the meal was particularly delightful. Everything you see comes from those times; it is all flavoured with remembrance; a pinch of the past, enough to season it but not enough to make it bitter.

"Consider a photograph; it is a picture of what was, a way of preserving memory. But this is much better! In this place, in our ghostly garden, our memories are made manifest; we can eat them and be filled with the joy we felt when we were alive."

She paused. "Though I daresay, although you will doubtless enjoy the meal, that it won't fill you up. The living cannot nourish themselves on memories," she said and whispered the last part, casting a nervous eye toward the head of the table.

"You keep looking so anxiously at her," Holly said. "Lady Arngrim, I mean. How come?"

"Hush now," said Mrs. Littlewood. "It would not do for her to find out you were… not like us," she said cautiously.

"Why not?" asked Adrian.

It was Holly who answered. "Because some ghosts miss being alive so much they'll do anything to live again, clinging on to anything that reminds them of life… like living people. That's what haunting is. It's a ghost who can't—or *won't*—let go of what used to be because they can't face what *is*."

Holly frowned at Lady Arngrim, who was still engrossed in her conversation and didn't notice. "She strikes me as just that type. So used to being the centre of attention that she can't stand that she isn't any more."

"Be that as it may," said Mrs. Littlewood, "It will not do to attract her attention on this subject, do you both understand? It could be most unpleasant. And I mean for *all* of us," she said, looking around the table at the other ghosts.

"Understood," said both Holly and Adrian at the same time.

"Well then, let's eat! I'm starving," Adrian said with feeling.

"You just had a jacket potato," Holly scoffed.

"That was ages ago. And then our lunch was put off, and here's a lunch sitting in front of us and I shan't wait a moment longer," he said as he helped himself to turkey and potatoes.

Holly rolled her eyes. "Boys and their stomachs," she said.

She eyed the table's contents. A dish she had not noticed before, but still somehow recognized, was sitting in front of her: A blue and white serving dish full of macaroni and cheese. "How'd that get there?" she asked. "That doesn't seem very British or whatever," she said.

"I'll wager it seems familiar to you, though, doesn't it?" winked Mrs. Littlewood.

"It looks like a dish we used to have, when I was little. It looks like…" Holly trailed off.

"Yes?" said Mrs. Littlewood merrily.

"Mom's macaroni and cheese," Holly said softly, as if not believing her own words.

"Just how you remember it, my dear, is it not?" asked Mrs. Littlewood.

"Yes, but how did you know—?" Holly began.

"I didn't, my dear. But all who sit at this table share their memories by sharing the meal, do you see? Think of it as a way of telling stories by partaking of the memory of your favourite food. Everyone takes a bite and is warmed and nourished by your memories of joy and comfort."

Holly eagerly began to fill her plate.

For his part, Adrian was even more determined now to sample as much as he could; for as hungry as he was, he was also eager for this new, unique experience.

His plate was filled with turkey, stuffing, potatoes, carrots, gravy; everything he could think of that was a proper feast. He gazed at the plate warmly; he then took a pitcher and filled his glass—and was overjoyed to discover that it was warm apple cider, the kind his parents let him have on very special occasions.

Taking a forkful, Adrian bit into the turkey; his mind filled with memories of Christmases past, of particularly good sauce and trimmings, of laughter and warmth and a sense of joyful anticipation. His mouth watered; the bite was exquisite, full of every good taste and nothing he did not desire.

"This is magic," he said.

Holly smiled through her mouthful of macaroni. "Special *proper* magic?" she asked.

Adrian closed his eyes, enjoying the moment of pure pleasure. "Precisely," he said.

The meal was lively, if such a word could be used, with cheerful conversation (Matthew told jokes, Miss Plumb sang a little song, Mr. Chakravarty told of his travels in life), and Mrs. Littlewood asked questions and complimented the others and kept the conversation going. It was a true *event,* as Holly would later call it. A real *occasion,* Adrian would agree.

However, neither of the cousins seemed to notice Lady Arngrim occasionally darting her eyes toward them, giving them shrewd, appraising looks from over the rim of her teacup. In fact, it wasn't until she spoke directly to them that they even realised she remembered they were there.

"Such polite children," Lady Arngrim said, eyeing them as a cat might eye a mouse; this made Holly and Adrian immediately uncomfortable.

"Er...thank you, Lady Arngrim," Adrian managed, nodding politely to her. *When in doubt,* he thought, *one must always rely on one's manners.*

"You've done such a delightful job of listening to your elders and remaining silent. Your behaviour has been impeccable," she said. Holly felt as if, although the words were complimentary, that they had somehow just been insulted.

The others at the table seemed to feel it, too; conversation had dwindled to nothing and now all eyes were on the Lady and the two cousins; it made both Holly and Adrian feel as if they were somehow being measured.

"But you must tell us something of yourselves. You remain something of a mystery! I recall you saying you'd only 'just arrived.' How came you here?"

There was a pause. Adrian glanced at Mrs. Littlewood who blinked rather deliberately at him; as if in warning, perhaps?

Holly remained silent as Adrian seemed to consider his answer. Finally, he said: "I'm sorry, Lady Arngrim...it's the strangest thing. I can't seem to remember."

The assembled company seemed to hold its breath awaiting Lady A's reaction to this; Holly imagined she could hear them all exhale at once with relief as the Lady laughed.

She waved her hand airily. "But of course, my boy, of course. Recent arrivals do tend to be a bit confused, after all. I'm sure it will all come rushing back to you at some point."

"Please, Lady," said Adrian. "I remember we were looking for our friend, Ethan Clarke. Have you seen him?" He looked around the table. "Have any of you?"

Holly silently applauded Adrian's audacity; it made sense, now that Lady A had started 'question period,' that Adrian could smoothly insert the question they'd come here to ask in the first place! She smiled prettily, looking innocently around the table.

It was Mr. Chakravarty who spoke: "Do you mean the boy who lives in the house up the lane from the cemetery? The quiet one?"

"Yes, the two-story house with the green shutters. Do you know it?"

"Yes, I suppose I do," mused Mr. Chakravarty. "A quiet boy. He sometimes takes walks by himself down the lane. Talks to himself at times. I see him go by the cemetery on occasion, when I think to notice. One doesn't always notice the living, after all."

There were murmurs of agreement around the table.

Adrian looked disappointed. "So nothing out of the ordinary, recently, like this week?"

Mr. Chakravarty seemed surprised by the question. "No, not as such. How do you mean, out of the ordinary?"

Lady Arngrim chimed in, her voice sweet and cold. "Yes, indeed. I daresay there hasn't been anything out of the ordinary in our—well, I suppose I could call it our *territory*—in ages." She fixed Holly and Adrian with an unnerving stare.

"Come to think of it," she said, and her voice now held a false lightness, belying its intensity: "I haven't heard or noticed anything at all around these parts that might disrupt the tranquility of our environment, or should I say our *domain*." Her eyes narrowed.

"Where did you say you were from, again?" she asked the cousins.

Holly would not allow herself to shy away from the woman's intense gaze. "Boston, Massachusetts, United States of America." she said confidently—almost defiantly, but a look from Mrs. Littlewood reminded her to keep herself in check.

Adrian followed suit: "Colchester, England."

"It seems so odd to me," said the Lady, "that two people from such different places should both find themselves arriving here at the same time," she said frostily.

"We're cousins," Adrian said. "Holly's family is visiting mine."

Lady Arngrim raised an eyebrow. "Is?" she asked.

Mrs. Littlewood cleared her throat. "I'm sure he meant "was." You know how new arrivals are-"

"Yes, thank you, Mrs. Littlewood," said Lady A, cutting her off. Mrs. Littlewood fell silent. "I am aware of the confusion of new arrivals. But what occurs to me is that, should two cousins have so recently passed over to our side, there'd have been quite a to-do, I should imagine. A *kerfuffle*, to use the vernacular. There'd have been grieving. Noise. Carrying-on.

"And yet these two—" and here she rose from her seat and began to walk around the table toward the cousins "—arrived without a whisper, without circumstance or occasion. Asking questions about the living, of all things."

She swept down the table towards them; Adrian and Holly stood, instinctively reaching for each other's hand for reassurance.

"Do you know, children, that new arrivals tend to voice their confusion by wondering where they are, where home is, where their loved ones are, that sort of thing? In short, they always appear lost, until one of us welcomes them and helps them sort themselves out. But you—dear me, but you both seemed quite calm and composed for people—*young* people, at that—who have so recently passed. So quiet, polite, not a single question until, of course, you asked about your friend.

"Not a family member or other loved one, mind. A *friend*. A lonely boy who keeps to himself. Most odd, indeed." And now her voice was quite tight, the steel behind her words no longer hidden behind silvery airs and laughter.

Holly was at a loss for words, and Adrian looked as though he was preparing to answer back when, suddenly, Lady Arngrim's hands shot out and grabbed them both by their wrists.

Her grip was as cold as ice, freezing and burning like a cruel winter where she touched, making their blood seem as if it too had chilled. They both cried out, almost in unison.

"You're warm!" she screamed. "You're alive!" She drew herself up to her full height, gripping them ever tighter, and began to wail, her voice a keening sound that hurt their ears as it tore through the clearing. "How have the living come here? How have you crossed over? Tell meeee!" she shrieked.

Holly screamed, if only to drown out the noise of the Lady's voice. Too, an odd wind had sprung up around the area, causing the decorations in the trees to jangle discordantly as lightning began to flash and thunder roared.

The other ghosts shrank back away from Lady Arngrim, who had undergone a transformation: no longer did she look like the serene, white-masked made-up noblewoman she had first appeared to be; now her dress was in tatters, her face sunken, giving her head a skull-like appearance beneath her powdered wig, and her eyes had gone dark, dark like pools of night staring the cousins down with rage and despair.

Mrs. Littlewood, struggling to keep her feet as the wind tore at her floral dress, shouted "Say nothing! Do not give her any more knowledge of you! She can use it to—"

Lady Arngrim turned her head and shrieked at Mrs. Littlewood, who vanished immediately.

"She's freezing our souls," Holly shouted over the wind. "We have to break free or we'll be dead for real!"

Desperately, Adrian glanced around for anything that might break the shrieking ghost's frozen-iron grip; he looked at the table, and narrowed his eyes in concentration—not an easy feat with the wind and the shrieking and the jangling all around him.

Holly saw the plates, cups, forks and knives begin to rise off the table and hurl themselves at the thing that had been Lady Arngrim. Pelted by the smaller objects, as the larger plates and platters smashed themselves against her head and skeletal arms, she shrieked again as she lost her grip.

"Run," came Mrs. Littlewood's voice from nowhere.

Still holding hands, the cousins ran back the way they'd come. Adrian was looking wildly for the triangular shape of the gate made by the trees, but could not see it; all he saw was more trees as they fled deeper into the ghostly woods, wind howling all around them.

"It should be close by," he said in confusion. "But I don't see it!"

"I can't see it, but I can feel it," Holly said after closing her eyes for a moment. "It's this way, come on!"

They both ran, Holly leading the way, as the shrieking followed them; there was a cold, silvery kind of light behind them as well, though neither dared to look back to see its source.

Then suddenly, as before, there was a kind of lurch—as if they had suddenly turned a corner—and there was the arch in front of them, and then they were through.

Holly tugged Adrian along. "Don't stop," she said. "Not until we're out of the cemetery."

Adrian said "You don't have to tell me twice," and they both ran past the rows of headstones until they had passed the gate—and back up the lane halfway to the house before they paused to catch their breath.

"I take it all back," Adrian said, panting. "The ghost world is very scary and I should never have asked you to do that and I am very very sorry," he said, his face pale and his eyes wide.

Holly nodded. "I've never been to the spirit world before. I didn't know what to expect, I just knew when she grabbed us—"

"—which was terrifying—" Adrian added—

"—that she was somehow draining us. Taking our life force. It's never happened before but I just somehow *knew*," Holly said, her gasping breaths eventually subsiding for more even ones.

"Then I think you just saved our lives," Adrian said, gulping as he, too, managed to calm down somewhat.

"If not for you and your throwing things at her, I think we'd still be back there," Holly said.

"Then we're a great team, we're still alive, and hurrah for us," Adrian said nervously.

"Yay for us," Holly agreed, and they laughed a little, a nervous kind of laugh that didn't feel quite true but nevertheless made them feel a bit better.

"I don't understand, though," Adrian said after a bit. "Why Lady A got so shirty with us. I mean, I only asked a question."

"Shirty?" asked Holly.

"Annoyed. Upset. Angry." Adrian explained.

"Oh, that. Well, remember how I told you that some ghosts are nice and some aren't?" Holly said.

"Yes? That much I saw for myself," Adrian said wryly.

"Yes, but there are reasons for it beyond just their personalities. Some ghosts crave life. They remember being alive and they want that feeling again. They're drawn to it, and they'd do anything to possess it." Holly explained.

"I don't understand," Adrian admitted. "If she wanted to be alive so much, why was she attacking us?"

"Because she saw or felt the life in us. Remember when she touched us and she was freezing? That was her trying to take our life, our energy, for herself. Remember when she changed into that...that thing? That's kind of a ghost's way of showing you its true form, its real personality. She was a Hunger Spirit, the kind of ghost that craves something it can't have, and it goes crazy if it sees its desire.

"In Lady A's case, what she desired most was to live again. Did you notice how she couldn't take her eyes off us during lunch? I think she must have sensed we were alive even before she knew it for sure."

Adrian digested this for a moment. "Can ghosts come back to life again?"

"I...don't think so," Holly said. "She wanted life, *our* life, but it wouldn't have helped her live again. She would have killed us and been left with nothing."

Adrian was quiet for a moment, then said, looking not at Holly but at the ground, "How do you know this?"

Holly put a hand on his arm. "If you're thinking I've experienced this before, I haven't. But ghosts talk. Some of them are friendly like Mrs. Littlewood, and they tell me things. When I was small they were very protective of me and told me how to watch myself around the bad ones. I don't know everything, but I've been told quite a bit. The rest I kind of figure out as I go."

Adrian whistled. "I think you're the bravest person I've ever met, growing up with ghosts like that all around you."

Holly took his hand. "I am pretty awesome," she said. This made Adrian laugh. "But seriously though, most of the time they're just like people. Experiences like today are few and far between, thank goodness."

"So that thing you said about ghosts showing up at the foot of your bed or acting out their death scenes in your Math class—" Adrian began.

"Yeah. Those two actually happened," Holly nodded. "They scared me a bit but at the same time, I was learning more about them and I knew they couldn't help what they were doing, you know? That's the part that's contrary: where the ghost half of them takes over, and they're not so much people anymore as… as… like, a circumstance, a series of events, or an emotion. They're like beasts, all raw instinct. And that can get pretty ugly, as we just saw."

"Wow," said Adrian, and then he repeated: "Wow." Then he frowned. "Mrs. Littlewood was trying to say something to us. 'Don't give her any more knowledge of you.' What did she mean by that?"

"Well, ghosts can be…clingy," Holly said carefully. "Like, for instance, I used to introduce myself by my name, but it was as if the ghosts could follow me around because they knew it. I stopped telling my name to people unless, say, my Mom or Dad were with me."

She sighed. "Now I'm kicking myself for the way we were introduced at lunch. She knows where we're from, and she knows our names."

"Does that mean she can find us?" Adrian asked worriedly.

"I guess so? I don't know what the rules are if we were in the spirit world, maybe it's different there. I really don't know."

"Well, at the very least, no one can say we didn't use our manners," Adrian joked. This made Holly giggle, which was echoed by Adrian.

Once they'd finished laughing (and shivering from a cold that was no longer there but that they still felt inside), Holly looked around. "Hang on. Have you noticed?"

"What?" Adrian said, looking around.

"We went in at lunchtime. But now—it's night."

And it was true. Streetlights were lit, the moon was high in the sky, visible through breaks in the clouds; it was definitely night, and quite late, at that.

"Oh, crumbs," said Adrian.

Chapter 7: The Empty House

"In all our searching, the only thing we've found that makes the emptiness bearable is each other."
—Carl Sagan

"What do we do now?" asked Holly. "Can you call your mum?" she said, looking around at the darkened lane.

"I don't have a phone. It wasn't considered 'a priority,' to quote my parents." Adrian sighed.

"Even though I hate cell phones, it sure would be useful right now," Holly admitted.

"Well, we can just go call at the Clarke house. We can ring my mum from there." Adrian said simply.

"I guess that's our only option," Holly agreed. "What time is it, anyway?"

Adrian looked at his watch. "Three in the afternoon, according to my watch. How can it be dark? We were only at Ghost Lunch for a little while."

"Yes, but we were in the ghost world, the spirit realm. Time is wonky around ghosts even on the living side of things; they kind of draw you into their time, and if you're too close to them for too long you kind of are brought into the little pocket world they carry around with them. So a couple of minutes to you might be a whole afternoon, or hours might be just a few moments. It doesn't make any sense."

"So we've definitely been missing for at least a few hours," Adrian said apprehensively.

"Assuming that this is even the same day we left," Holly said. "I don't know. I've never gone this far before."

Adrian hid his face in his hands for a moment. "My mother is going to murder me."

"My parents aren't exactly going to be happy when they find out, either," Holly said ruefully.

"We need a story. Something they can believe, since we obviously can't tell them the truth," Holly said.

"We could say we went walking and got lost?" Adrian said, thinking out loud. "It is essentially the truth," he mused.

"Would your mom believe you got lost? You can see for miles around here, and this is a small town. Why wouldn't we have just asked for directions?"

"We were tired and fell asleep?" Adrian suggested.

"Eeeeh," Holly said, a noise of negation. "I don't know. Let me try to think of something. I'm usually good at covering up ghost-related weirdness."

"By all means, have a go," Adrian said. "But be quick, because we're almost there." And he pointed ahead of them.

Just up the lane from where they were walking sat the Clarke residence, windows dark on both floors and with the noted absence of cars in the drive—including Adrian's mother's.

"It doesn't look like anyone's home," said Holly.

"Maybe everyone's asleep," said Adrian, looking around the neighbourhood. "I don't see any lights on in any other houses." And indeed, the street was lined with equally dark and silent homes.

"It is super creepy here at night," Holly whispered. "I'm used to big city noise. Here it's just so quiet. Like really, though, it's *too* quiet."

"Agreed. I hadn't noticed, but then I'm usually asleep at this time—I think. Are you sure we're not still in the spirit realm?" he asked, looking around.

"Positive. This is just earthly creepiness, not ghostly." But that didn't make either of them feel any better.

They arrived at the front door of the Clarkes'. Adrian gathered up his courage and rang the bell. "Have you thought of an excuse yet?" he asked Holly.

"We fell asleep. I don't have anything better than that." she admitted.

"All right then," Adrian said, and they waited for someone to answer the door.

And they waited.

And waited.

"How can there be nobody home?" Holly asked, trying to peer in a darkened window. "Or did they not hear the bell?"

"It occurs to me that perhaps they aren't sleeping here?" Adrian mused. "I mean, if they're trying to sell their home, maybe they stay at a hotel or something so the place stays clean?"

"But you'd think, with their son missing, they'd be here in case he tried to come home?" Holly countered.

"Maybe the police told them to stay away, perhaps like it was a crime scene and needed to be kept clear?"

Holly gaped at Adrian. "Crime scene? Jeepers, Adrian! Do you always go for the creepiest explanation?"

"Well I don't know!" Adrian said, frustrated. "The fact remains that there is no one at home."

"Then how are we supposed to contact your parents? Start ringing random doorbells in the middle of the night?" Holly said, throwing up her hands.

"Well...we could still go into this house, I mean, if no one's home, no one will know we've been here." Adrian said.

"Except that the door is locked," Holly pointed out.

"I know a trick for that," Adrian said.

Holly cocked her head. "Are you saying you're going to pick the lock?"

Adrian grinned impishly at her. "Not exactly."

Holly saw him kneel down, inspecting the doorknob. He put his hands flat against the door on either side of it, and appeared to be staring at it. Suddenly, there was a click and the sound of a bolt being drawn back, and the door creaked open.

"Clickety-click," he said with another grin as he stood up and brushed off his trousers.

"Nice trick," said Holly admiringly. "You're well on your way to becoming one of those really interesting unsavoury people with questionable skills," she said.

"My questionable skill has just got us shelter and access to a phone. So, you're welcome," he said wryly.

"I was only kidding. That was super cool. Now let's get inside before someone sees us," Holly said, entering the house.

Adrian looked around; there certainly didn't seem to be anyone else who was awake and outside at this hour—but nevertheless followed Holly inside.

One of the first things Adrian realised was that Holly was not afraid of the dark. He found this odd, considering all the unseen things that she must know could hide in it. When he asked her about it, she said "That's just it. If there were someone or something here, I could sense it—hear it, see it lurking in the shadows or whatever. But there's nothing, so—it's just a house."

As if to give the lie to her statement, a groaning sound echoed from upstairs, as if some great creature had moaned in its sleep; the wood of the house seemed to creak as if under an immense weight.

"And what, pray tell, was that?!?" Adrian asked, trying to stop panic from rising in his voice.

"I don't know. Ghosts moan, but it's people-moans. Not groaning house moans. Maybe it's wind?" She sounded doubtful.

"There wasn't a trace of a breeze outside. It sounded like it came from upstairs."

"Maybe Mrs. Clarke is actually here and she snores?" Holly said weakly.

Adrian sighed. "That was not a snore," he said regretfully. "I wish it had been. I wish we could turn on the lights."

"We don't dare, in case someone sees. Then we'd have to explain how we got inside here and we're already behind on believable explanations." Holly said.

"Then perhaps we'd better go see what that noise was, and eliminate all this guesswork," Adrian suggested.

"After you," Holly said, gesturing, although he could barely see her in the dim light streaming in the windows from the streetlights outside.

They proceeded up the stairs quietly, in single file, having quite forgotten about calling Adrian's mother.

As they ascended the staircase, Adrian said "I used to have dreams about empty, dark houses at night. I would look at their windows and imagine they were great dark eyes. If you looked into them too long you'd be pulled inside and be trapped in the darkened house forever."

Holly whispered, "Is now really the best time to be telling that story?"

"It just popped into my head," Adrian said defensively. "You must admit the situation is appropriate for it."

"Not when we're inside a dark house that I most definitely want to leave as soon as possible," Holly shot back. "And shh! We should be quiet."

"If there were anyone here they'd have heard us come in. It's a little late to be circumspect."

"Really? *Circumspect*? You couldn't just say '*careful*' or '*cautious*'?" Holly snorted.

"I talk when I get nervous. And the words kind of come out...big. Sorry."

"I want to tell you there's nothing to be nervous about, but considering what we're doing, that would be a lie," Holly said.

They reached the upstairs landing and peered down the dark hall. Ethan's bedroom door was open, pale white light shining in from the street lamps outside.

Holly stopped. "I feel something," she said.

"A ghost?" Adrian asked, his heart sinking. He'd had quite enough of them for one day.

"No, but like...something. Like we're being watched." Holly looked around, but saw nothing. "But there's nobody here."

"If it isn't a ghost, then how can you sense it?" Adrian asked. "Or do you just mean you feel apprehensive?"

Holly sighed. "No, I don't feel any more *afraid, jittery* or *jumpy* than is normal for being in someone else's empty house in the middle of the night. Seriously, calm down with the big words."

Adrian mumbled "Sorry. Can't help it."

Holly took his hand. "Let's go to Ethan's room. I'm getting a feeling it's coming from there."

"D'you think he could have come home?" Adrian asked.

"I think we'd have woken him up by now," Holly said, and upon reaching Ethan's doorway, peered inside.

The room was as it had been before: tidy, but empty. During the day, it had been nice, if a bit bland. But at night, every shadow seemed sinister, and filled the cousins with a sense of foreboding.

"It feels different in here," Adrian said. "Maybe I'm just feeling creeped out in general."

"Now who's apprehensive?" Holly said.

"Ha ha," Adrian said without mirth.

"No, but you're right," Holly relented. "I had the same feeling and now I'm sure of it; there's something in here. Or at least, the feeling is coming from here. It's like… like some huge animal is breathing. I don't know how else to say it."

"You can hear breathing?" Adrian asked, looking this way and that.

"Not literally," Holly struggled to explain. "I just… feel something."

Adrian was looking around the room. "I feel something too but I'm assuming it's just my nerves because I'm in a strange house in the middle of the night."

Then he gasped.

"What?" Holly said, turning to see what had caught Adrian's attention.

Adrian pointed; against the wall near the door was a full-length mirror, the kind one used to dress, to look themselves over from head to toe. It was framed in brass and stood on the floor in an antique-looking wooden stand.

"Have you noticed the mirror?" Adrian asked.

"What about it?" Holly said, looking at it.

"We're not in it," Adrian pointed—and sure enough, the mirror showed the room but not the two children standing in front of it.

The two approached the mirror until they were standing directly in front of it. Indeed, the mirror showed only the room behind them; it was as if Holly and Adrian were simply not there.

Holly waved her hand uselessly in front of the mirror. Nothing.

"How can we be directly in front of it and not be in it? I mean, it shows the room—" Adrian began.

Holly frowned. "Whatever I'm feeling, it's coming from this," she said. "I feel… lonely. Empty. All alone."

Adrian put a hand on Holly's shoulder. "Are you okay?" he asked.

"Mostly," she answered. She rubbed her hands together as if she were cold. "It just feels creepy. Like watching someone cry, you feel bad for them but you don't know what you can say or do to help."

Adrian nodded. Curiously, he leaned forward and breathed a heavy, warm breath on the mirror; it fogged up instantly. "So we can fog it up," he said. "Clearly, we're here and we can affect it, we just can't see ourselves in it—"

"Look!" Holly said as she pointed. On the edge of where Adrian had breathed was the letter P, as if someone else had fogged up the mirror and drawn on it with their finger.

"P?" Adrian questioned. He breathed on the mirror again, exhaling until he had revealed the entirety of what had been written:

ꟼⱢƎH

The cousins gasped.

"HELP," Adrian said. "But it's written weird, sort of reversed, like—"

"—like it was written from the other side of the mirror," Holly said breathlessly.

"How can that be possible?" Adrian wondered, reaching out to touch the letters, his fingers brushing the foggy surface of the mirror.

"Adrian, don't—" Holly began, but too late.

Adrian had vanished. She was alone.

Chapter 8: The Mirror

*"The mirror crack'd from side to side; "The curse
is come upon me," cried The Lady of Shalott."*
—Alfred Lord Tennyson

Adrian found himself standing alone in Ethan's bedroom, quite disoriented. He had been facing the mirror but now it was...gone?

He blinked and noticed he had somehow got turned around; the mirror was now at his back.

But that wasn't all. The room was somehow *wrong*; it made him feel dizzy even as he looked around at it.

And then it came to him: *Of course. Everything in here is in reverse—mirrored. It only makes sense if—*

—if I'm now on the other side of the mirror, he realised.

He took a deep breath and tried not to panic. *It's no problem,* he thought, *Holly is just on the other side and she can help figure this out.*

Even as he thought it, Holly suddenly appeared beside him, gasping as if she had just been running. "Adrian! Oh jeez. Oh wow. You just disappeared and I didn't know what to do so I just put my hand on the mirror and then I felt this pulling and I fell forward and I thought I was going to fall but then here you are and—"

"It's okay, it's okay," Adrian said and hugged her. "We're both all right. We're okay."

Holly took a moment to catch her breath. "Okay. Just… wow. Don't ever go and just touch something creepy again, okay? You never know what could happen."

Adrian looked around ruefully. "Well, I know one thing that can happen."

"Right," Holly agreed, looking around. "Everything's backward. We must be on the other side of the mirror."

"Exactly my thought. Can we get back?" Adrian asked.

"We should be able to, if we just touch the—" Holly reached out and placed her hand flat against the cold glass of the mirror.

Nothing happened.

"Oh oh." She said in a small voice. "I thought that it worked both ways, coming and going but… something's in the way. Like I'm being blocked."

"Blocked?" Adrian asked.

"Remember when we went through the tree arch in the graveyard and there was that sudden left turn feeling? That was a gate, a hole, a door between our world and the spirit world. I felt the same thing when I…when I sort of fell through the mirror," Holly explained. "Although it felt weird, like, backwards compared to the graveyard door which I guess only makes sense," she said.

"But now it feels like the door is closed. And more than that, it feels like it's being held shut. I push and push but the door won't open."

Holly looked solemnly at Adrian.

"I think we're stuck here."

"How does that work?" asked Adrian. "We got in, how is it we can't get out? Can't you do some…I don't know… some ghosty thing?"

Holly shot him a withering look. "Listen, *thicko*, I can only see ghosts and…and feel stuff, okay? What you're asking for is some kind of hocus-pocus I can't do. I need you to focus on the here and now, okay?"

"Right," said Adrian. He grinned at Holly in spite of himself. "You called me a thicko."

"Wasn't that the proper usage of the term?" Holly asked sweetly.

"It was perfect," Adrian said, and they both laughed.

"Okay but seriously," said Adrian, regaining his composure. "Where in heaven's name are we?"

Holly mused. "I think we can agree that we're in the spirit world again," she said.

"But how can that be?" Adrian asked, bewildered. "You said you didn't see any ghosts."

"No, but remember what Mrs. Littlewood said?" Holly reminded him. "'*There are more spirits than just the ghosts of the dearly departed*'," she said, managing a passable imitation of the lady ghost.

"Maybe the mirror had a spirit, and through it we can access the spirit world," Holly mused.

"Mirrors can have spirits?" Adrian narrowed his eyes as he studied the mirror again.

"Well, think about it. You always hear stories about weird things happening around mirrors. Seeing people out of the corner of your eye, but when you turn around they're not there. Covering mirrors after someone dies. Using mirrors to see things the way you'd use a crystal ball."

"That's called 'divination,'" Adrian said.

"Thank you, Oxford English Dictionary, may I continue?" Holly said. Adrian frowned at her, but nodded grumpily.

"So if there are all these legends and myths about the power of mirrors, why couldn't some of them be true? Maybe mirrors really are magic gateways to the spirit world."

"I've believed that mirrors were magic ever since I read *Alice Through The Looking-Glass*," Adrian said. "I always thought: 'Of course there's another world on the mirror's other side, if only I could get there,' but now it seems as if it's all real, it's all true."

"Except that this isn't Wonderland," Holly said ruefully.

"So, if mirrors are gates to the spirit world," Adrian said thoughtfully, "wouldn't you have noticed that by now? I mean, you're sensitive to these things."

"Hm. That's a good point. But I'm discovering a lot of new things on this trip. ghost tea service, ghost gardeners and tea parties and getting attacked by a real Hunger Spirit. Maybe I'm just noticing for the first time because so much is happening?"

Adrian nodded. "That makes sense," he said. "So then... to figure out how to get out of here and back to the real world, it would follow that we have to better understand the rules of... of the mirror, I guess... to learn how to open the door again?"

Holly pondered a moment. "That sounds logical," she decided. "You know, you've got a knack for focussing on problem-solving—once you're done freaking out about it, that is."

"Oh thank you," Adrian said drily. He looked around the room. "Okay. So, we know we can't get back through the mirror. Perhaps the mirror is only an 'in' door and we need to find the 'out'?"

"Sure," Holly said, shrugging. "Your guess is as good as mine." Then she frowned. "But I need to tell you something first. That feeling I had? That feeling of being watched? It's stronger here. It's all around. It's not just the mirror, it's...everywhere."

Adrian sighed and couldn't help but shiver a little. "Well, we'll just have to make do," which was something his mother always said when things weren't working out properly.

"And…" Holly said hesitantly.

"Yes?" Adrian prompted.

Holly folded her arms across her chest as if for warmth. "I feel sadness. Loneliness. It's such a big feeling, all around us like the being-watched feeling. I feel like I want to cry, it's so bad."

Adrian looked at her with concern. "You're not alone," he said, and hugged her.

"I know, I know," she said, but she did not attempt to break the hug or move away. "It's not my feeling. It's someone else's. And it's so strong here."

Adrian stepped back, his eyes wide. "Wait a minute. Sad and lonely? Do you suppose…?"

Holly knew what he meant instantly.

"Ethan!" they both said in unison.

"Maybe he fell through the mirror too, and can't find his way out!" Adrian said excitedly.

"Maybe he's still here!" Holly added.

Emboldened with purpose, the two cousins joined hands. "Let's go look for him, then," Adrian said and opened the bedroom door which for some reason was shut.

"I don't remember shutting this door," he murmured as he opened it.

"Maybe not everything on this side is the exact mirror of our side," said Holly. "Let's just go find Ethan—if he's here—and figure out a way back!"

"Let's do that," Adrian said, and together they stepped out into the hall.

Right away they noticed differences; the hall was at an odd angle, as if the whole thing was a picture that had been hung crookedly on a wall; and yet they didn't slide down the floor or fall over (though it was certainly a dizzying effect!); they kept their feet and, as they walked slowly forward, the hallway seemed to orient itself to them—or perhaps it was they who oriented to the floor?

Adrian looked behind them. "Whoa," he said. Holly looked too; the bedroom door was now high on the wall almost to the ceiling. It seemed the further they walked down the hall away from where they'd been, the more warped the place became.

"Does this hall seem a lot longer to you than it is in the real world?" Adrian asked Holly.

"I know that spirit perceptions are warped when they come to our world," Holly answered. "Sometimes they just can't see things as they are, or they only see them as they used to be, or as they expect them to be. Perception is really skewed when you compare the living to the dead, so I expect the spirit world would be the same to us. We're alive, so we can't see this world as it truly is, just as we expect it to be."

Adrian gritted his teeth. "You know, all those books about kids going on adventures never mention weird stuff like this. It's all golden chalices and friendly dragons and talking animals and it's never getting lost in a mirror ghost spirit house."

"Pity," Holly said with feeling. "It'd be nice if all of this stuff had some kind of manual that came with it."

"No kidding," Adrian said, and they continued up the hall.

All the doors were closed. They opened each in turn and revealed a closet, which was empty; a bathroom, and what they assumed was Ethan's parents' bedroom, and what appeared to be an empty spare room.

"So Ethan isn't in any of the upstairs rooms. Where would he be?" Holly asked.

"If it were me," Adrian said, "I'd be trying to find a way to get back. And if the mirror in the bedroom didn't work—"

"—you'd try to find another mirror!" Holly finished.

Excitedly they returned to the bathroom, which had a mirrored medicine cabinet above the sink. Strangely, the mirror was black.

Holly pressed her hand to it, but nothing happened.

"Still blocked?" Adrian asked.

"No, it's like… if the first mirror felt like a door, then this feels like a wall," Holly answered. "Like it isn't meant to open. It's just a mirror."

"I suppose not all mirrors are doors," Adrian sighed. "Perhaps that's why it's black? Like my vision of a house with dark eyes; dark mirrors aren't open, they're closed."

Holly shivered. "And in your house-vision, if you look too long into them, you get trapped inside," she said.

"Oh, what a time to bring that up," Adrian said. "But the first mirror wasn't black," he mused. "Maybe if black mirrors mean 'closed,' normal mirrors mean 'open?'"

"Then we need to find out if there are other mirrors in the house," Holly said. "Don't give up."

"Give up? Never!" Adrian rallied and took her hand. "We're going to find Ethan and we're going to find a way out of here, so there," he said firmly.

"So there," Holly echoed.

They checked Ethan's parents' room and found a dresser with a big round mirror affixed to the top of it, but it too was black. They moved on to the spare room; but the spare room was, as they had discovered before, quite empty.

"This floor is clear, shall we move on?" Adrian asked. Holly nodded silently.

Cautiously they made their way back down the hallway to the stairwell, and began to descend to the main floor.

As they made their way to the landing, Adrian mused, "Might Ethan have tried to leave the house? Perhaps go next door, try to get someone's attention?"

Holly looked at the front door. "I have a feeling if he did, it didn't work."

Adrian opened the door and looked outside. "Huh," he said. "What?" Holly asked, joining him.

From the doorway they could see the front steps of the house, and the little lane that led into the front yard and the little fence that bordered the property—but beyond that was obscured by a thick, white fog.

"It was nighttime when we came in. Now it's…daytime? But with fog," Adrian observed, confused.

"I don't know if it's daytime or nighttime," Holly said. "More like 'no' time. Like time doesn't matter here."

Adrian gestured to the fog. "But clearly, there's weather here. Perhaps when the fog clears we could see where Ethan might have gone?"

Holly rubbed her arms as if she were cold. "I think if Ethan went into that fog, he'd be lost," she said. "I mean really *lost*. I think if we were to step into it, we'd lose our way and be trapped in the spirit world forever."

"Whoa," Adrian said nervously. "Why do you say that?"

"Remember I told you ghosts sometimes tell me stories?" Holly began. "One thing they all agree on is the fog. Fog surrounds their world. If they're attached to a house, or a place—then they can only see that place, and everything else is fog. If they're attached to a person, they can only see that person and what's immediately around them, otherwise it's all fog.

"It's like a boundary, or border, or wall between the various little worlds that spirits live in. Like, you couldn't just walk down the lane from this house to the cemetery and find the forest party place. The worlds aren't…aren't *connected*," Holly struggled to explain.

"It's all separated by this fog they all describe. Those that go into the fog never come back. That's what they all tell me."

"That's… rather an important safety tip," Adrian said, visibly paler now. He swallowed. "So, let's just assume Ethan did not walk into the fog, because if he did, it's hopeless. Let's assume he's still somewhere in the house. Only…" he trailed off, lost in thought.

"Hello?" Holly said, irritated. Adrian blinked at her. "I hate when you do that, go inside your head like that. 'Only' what?" she asked with frustration.

"I was just thinking, only if he's still in the house, why hasn't he called out or come out to see us? Surely he'd have heard us traipsing around by now," Adrian offered.

"I don't think so. Haven't you noticed how sound doesn't seem to carry, here? Even our footsteps on the stairs were silent, like all the vibrations from any noise just kind of die as soon as they're made."

"I wish you hadn't said 'die,'" Adrian groaned. "But all right. So we assume he can't hear us, and we can't hear him. So we search until we find him."

"Pretty much," Holly said.

They closed the front door, shutting out the fog (which calmed them both considerably) and began searching the main floor. The sitting room held a mirror above the fireplace, but it too was black.

Adrian noticed a television in the room. "The screen is reflective, does it count as a mirror?" he asked.

"One, it's technology, like, electronic and not...um... natural? Is the only way I can think to describe it. Spirits don't really like technology because it kind of goes haywire around them, so I don't think a TV could be of any use as a spirit portal. At least, that's what I'm guessing. Two, it's black too. See?"

"That makes sense. All right. So, not this room either," he said.

Neither did the kitchen or the front room offer any options.

"Did you notice the kitchen had food in it?" Adrian asked Holly.

"Yes, most kitchens do, why?" Holly answered.

"But isn't it strange," Adrian mused. "That there'd be food on this side of the mirror. I mean, everything here is kind of...inert, like the way you describe the deadening of noise. Why have food in a mirror image?"

"Well, logically, everything from the real world would be mirrored here," Holly pointed out.

"Exactly. But the Clarkes are selling this house. Why, then, is the kitchen fully stocked?"

Holly paused to consider. "That is a really good question."

"It's as if…" Adrian swallowed. "As if the house is providing for someone living here. To keep them fed."

"Ethan." Holly said. "You're saying the house is making sure Ethan is fed?"

Adrian's eyes went wide with realisation. "That…that *is* what I'm saying! Remember what Mrs. Littlewood said: *'There are more spirits than just the ghosts of the dearly departed!'* We've been repeating what she said but not understanding it! Holly, *the house is a spirit!* Or has a spirit, or however it works but the house is…aware!" he exclaimed.

Holly froze. Both she and Adrian looked around, now suddenly nervous about their surroundings.

Holly spoke aloud, working it out in her mind as she talked herself through it: "That's why I had all those strong feelings when we were in Ethan's room, and why they were stronger after we came through the mirror," she said. "I was sensing a spirit, only not a ghost…I was feeling what *the house itself* feels."

She looked nervously around. "And what it feels is… *desperate*. It doesn't want its people, I mean the people that live in it, to leave. Adrian…" she said apprehensively, her voice dropping to a whisper.

"I don't think Ethan just accidentally fell into the mirror. I think the house *took him.* And," and now her voice was so quiet even Adrian had to strain to hear her:

"I think it means to keep him."

Chapter 9: The Lonely House

"It seems to me we can never give up longing and wishing ...there are certain things we feel to be beautiful and good, and we must hunger for them."
—George Eliot

Adrian and Holly slowly continued their search for Ethan, but now they held hands and tried to focus on being brave when the truth was they were much more scared than they had been.

They didn't speak much, so afraid they were of the house hearing them and not sure what it was capable of; they silently agreed that perhaps they shouldn't speak their plans out loud, lest the house somehow notice them and choose to thwart them.

Down the hallway from the kitchen, it seemed to warp and bend more intensely than even the upstairs; it was as if their surroundings had gone from house to madhouse.

Adrian finally broke the silence. "This won't work if we can't even talk to each other," he said, exasperated but still cautiously quieter than usual. "Why is this hallway so strange—well, I mean compared with the other strangeness we've already seen?"

"I don't know," said Holly. "Maybe it's trying to confuse us?"

"It's doing a good job," Adrian grumbled. "Trying to figure out its purpose is like watching a fish climb a tree. Nothing makes sense—here!" he exclaimed.

Holly saw what Adrian had just seen: a door had appeared on the wall next to them.

"A magical appearing door?" Adrian mused.

Holly had a sudden recollection. "Wait. Step back a bit." She said. As one, they both stepped backward.

The door vanished.

Holly nodded, as if this confirmed something. "Now forward again." They both stepped forward.

The door reappeared.

"It's like a reverse mirage," Adrian said. "You can only see it when you're close to it."

"No, it's like your garden, don't you see? The door is there, but you can't notice it until you're standing right in front of it!"

Adrian's eyes widened in understanding. "I get it! But why this door and not any of the others? If it's like my garden—" he began.

"—then there must be something behind it worth protecting," Holly finished.

"Ethan!" they both exclaimed.

Adrian tried the door. "Locked," he said. "But not for long."

He knelt on the floor and stared directly at the keyhole underneath the doorknob. As with the main door to the house, he concentrated, and then Holly heard the "click" of the lock and Adrian stood, and pulled the door open.

"Oh nice one!" Holly said, peering around him to see what was beyond the door: a wooden stairway leading down into blackness. "Oh great," she said.

"Every scary story just *has* to have a cellar in it," groaned Adrian. "And us without a torch."

Holly looked at him. "That's British for 'flashlight,' right?"

Adrian huffed, "'Flashlight' is American for 'torch.'"

Holly rolled her eyes. "So what do we do, just go down into the blackness?

"Not a chance," Adrian said. "But wait—perhaps if the kitchen is stocked, there might be a tor—a *flashlight*—in a drawer somewhere. Or perhaps a candle, or something?"

"Worth a look," Holly said. "Let's go back to the kitchen."

As it happened, they were in luck. In a drawer in the kitchen was a flashlight, and when they pressed the button it actually worked; light sprang forth and helped them to see better in the house's strange half-light.

"Well, it's a very practical house, if nothing else," Adrian said.

"I guess. I keep thinking it just heard what we were talking about and then just conjured up what we asked for," Holly said.

"I want a motorcycle," Adrian said.

Nothing happened.

"Just checking," he grinned. Holly gave him a wry look, but they were both feeling better now that they had some light, even after they returned to the strange cellar door.

"I guess we just go down and…and look?" Adrian seemed to ask Holly.

Holly nodded. "It's not like we've got many options," she said.

Adrian went in front, holding the torch, and Holly came behind. She put her hand on his shoulder, partly so she wouldn't lose him in the dark, and partly to comfort them both so they could feel connected to each other.

At the bottom of the stairs was a cellar room, all concrete and unfurnished, but with boxes piled here and there as if the room had been forgotten for years. A casement window shone a weak, pale light on the floor in a rectangle shape.

Directly under the window was a metal box that seemed built into the floor. It had no top. Holly's brow wrinkled and she said, "What in the world is that?"

Adrian frowned, concentrating. "I think…" he said, remembering, "…that it's an old coal or wood box, from back in the days when houses were heated by coal or wood stoves? I think the window is probably where the delivery chute used to be. People would deliver the week's supply of whatever and just dump it down the chute into the box, and it would be put in the furnace?"

"Okay, cool," said Holly. "Shine the light in the box. This is the point in the scary story where something jumps out at us."

Adrian directed the flashlight's beam into the box; it was empty.

But it was then that they heard the whimpering; coming from behind the box, underneath the window. A quiet sobbing, as if someone were crying but trying very hard to be quiet.

"Hello?" Adrian said.

"Ethan?" Holly said. "Is that you?"

From behind the box, a head peeked out over the top; then, slowly standing up, a boy revealed himself from the spot where he had been hidden: apparently the same age as Adrian and Holly, with brown hair and thoughtful brown eyes. He looked dishevelled, his clothes wrinkled and dirty, and it seemed as though he hadn't been sleeping.

"Who are you?" he asked, his voice halting as he tried not to cry.

"I'm Holly, and this is Adrian," said Holly. "You're Ethan, right? Ethan Clarke?"

"Yes," said the boy simply.

"We've come looking for you. We're going to get you home. I mean, your real home, not…whatever this is."

Holly had a sudden sinking feeling. A boy alone in a cellar, crying, could very well be a ghost. She turned to Adrian. "You can see him, right?"

Adrian nodded. "He's real." Holly sighed with relief.

"Are *you* real?" Ethan asked. "You're not some trick?"

Adrian explained how they had been visiting the house with his mother, and had been allowed into his room—and here he simply said that they touched the mirror and fell into it, avoiding the topic of ghosts and midnight excursions altogether.

"We had only just heard you were missing, then we found ourselves here, so now we're going to get you out," he finished.

Holly privately thought that Adrian was a bad liar, but Ethan gave no sign that he noticed.

"It's not going to let us out," Ethan said, sadly. "I tried the front door. It wouldn't open. It kept moving things around, trying to get me to stay inside. I tried the windows, and I couldn't open them. I couldn't even break them. I came down here because it was the only place I didn't feel it watching me.

"Sometimes I sneak up to the kitchen for food. I don't know what day it is. I don't know how long I've been here. I just want to go home," Ethan said, his eyes filling with tears once more. "But it won't let me go. Now you're here and you won't be able to go, either."

As if to underscore Ethan's point, they suddenly jumped as they heard a loud bang as the door at the top of the stairs slammed shut.

Ethan shivered. "See? It won't let us out. It wants to keep us here!" he said.

Adrian, for his part, had gone past scared and was now angry. Spirits and ghosts seemed to think they could do whatever they wanted, and just now he wasn't having it.

"We'll see about that. Come on," he said and led the way up the stairs. Holly once again put her hand on his shoulder, and extended her other hand to Ethan, who took it.

"You'll never get through," Ethan said. "Not while it's holding the door closed. I've tried."

Adrian peered at the lock, concentrating. "It's not locked," he said. "It's like you described the mirror," he said to Holly. "Something is holding the door shut."

"It's the house," said Ethan. "It's like the door is a part of its body, and it's flexing a muscle to keep it closed."

Holly nodded. "That makes sense. A spirit has control over itself, so it probably can move things around if it wants."

Ethan looked puzzled. "A spirit?"

Holly didn't feel like getting into all of that at that moment, so she said, "Well, like, if the house is alive, I mean, it's not an animal and it's not a person, so like…it's a spirit," she attempted to explain.

Ethan, tired and frightened, seemed at that point to accept whatever Holly and Adrian said, which made the whole thing a bit easier.

Holly thought he'd been through quite enough without having to add magic and ghosts and portals to Ethan's already-confused mind. However, they were now faced with the very real problem of the closed door. If they couldn't open it, how were they to find an exit from this mirror-spirit world?

Adrian pushed and pounded on the door to no avail. "Stupid house, let us go!" he shouted. There was no answer.

"Right!" Adrian shouted. He turned back to the other two, and Holly saw in the flashlight that his face was beet red with fury. "Everyone stand back," he said.

Holly looked at him. "What are you going to do?" she asked him.

"I'm going to push the door open," he said.

"It's no use," Ethan lamented. "I've tried. Threw my whole body against it and it wouldn't budge an inch."

"I have a…better method of pushing than that," Adrian said, looking meaningfully at Holly.

Holly nodded. "Are you strong enough?" she asked.

"I don't know," Adrian said. "But I'll tell you this: I've never 'pushed' while being this angry before! So I guess we'll see." And he sounded determined.

Holly turned to Ethan. "Let's wait at the bottom of the stairs," she said, more to distract Ethan from what was happening than to give Adrian room; years of having to protect her secret from the people around her had taught her that everything was just easier if no one knew exactly what was going on. Trying to explain that Adrian could move things with his mind might just put Ethan over the edge from "upset" to "traumatised," and that was something she still hoped to avoid despite being trapped.

Meanwhile, Adrian was breathing heavily, working himself up. He was angry at the house, angry at its apparently unthinking, covetous behaviour; like a child, it missed Ethan and wanted him so it thought it could just *have* him—and he and Holly as well! Well, that wouldn't do. No, it wouldn't do at all!

He drew in his breath and let it out in a great shout—yelling at the door and willing it with all his might to open, pushing with his mind, with his power, with the full force of his will—

—There was a splintering sound, and the door exploded outward, blowing off its hinges and smashing against the opposite wall.

Adrian dropped to his knees, panting. His ears were ringing. His head was throbbing. "So there," he said. "Rotten house."

There arose a loud moaning that echoed throughout the house, a mournful sound that filled the hallways and echoed even into the cellar.

Holly pulled Ethan up the stairs with her as she checked on Adrian. "Are you all right?" she asked. "We've got to get moving. The tone of the house has changed. It doesn't feel lonely any more. It feels *angry!*"

Ethan looked at the broken door lying on the hallway floor. "You broke the door. How did you—?"

Adrian got slowly to his feet. "Stronger than I look," he managed.

Holly was pleased that he had chosen to keep his secret, but had other things to think about just now. "Listen," she said to both boys, "We have got to get out of here. If the house is like a prison when it's sad, I don't want to know what it's like when it's angry!"

"Where do we go?" Adrian asked. "The fog—"

"Not outside. Back up to Ethan's room. It's the only mirror that's a portal!" Holly said. "We have to figure out a way to get it open because it's the only way we've seen to get back!"

All three of them began to head for the stairwell upstairs, but the house seemed to twist, the hallways becoming dizzy spirals, playing with their perception of reality. "Don't think about what you see," Holly shouted over the house's moaning. "Just keep your feet on the floor and keep moving forward!"

She was right; as long as they slid their feet towards their goal, they kept moving forward. It seemed the house's twisting and strangeness was mere illusion, playing tricks with their sight without being real.

At last they reached the staircase, and began to climb—but then they heard a scraping noise from the top, and a rumbling—a table from the upstairs hallway was tumbling toward them, apparently attempting to knock them back downstairs.

Adrian gestured, and the table flew off the stairs to the side, crashing onto the main room's floor below.

"The house has gone crazy! It's trying to kill us!" Ethan yelled.

"It's trying to keep us here any way it can," Holly said. "I think we have the right idea, going back to your room. Have you been back there since you came here?"

Ethan shook his head, clinging tightly to the railing. "The door's been closed. I couldn't get in. I slept on the couch in the sitting room."

"Then we're definitely on the right track," Holly said. "Adrian!" she shouted over the roar of the house's anger, "We've got to get to Ethan's room!"

"On it," Adrian said as he made his way to the top of the stairs.

Immediately a huge wind sprang up out of nowhere, howling down the hallway, pushing the trio away from Ethan's room. Holly shouted "Seriously?" at nothing in particular.

Straining, Adrian held up a hand. In his mind, he pictured a wedge shape—narrow at the front and wide at the back—surrounding the three of them. Immediately the wind died down, even though it screamed past them on either side, rocking pictures hanging on the wall, blowing them off the wall, causing small rugs on the floor to blow away down the hall.

They inched forward toward the door.

Adrian said to Holly: "I don't know if I can do another door," he said fearfully. "I've never used the power this much before. It's all I can do to block the wind—"

But just then, Holly pointed at Ethan's door. "Look!" she said, as the door swung open.

"Go!" she said, and the three sprinted into the room, turning to slam the door behind them, shutting out the wind.

The room was eerily silent in the aftermath, but there was an odd, cold glow illuminating the room.

"Greetings, children. I have found you again at last," said a silvery voice with iron in it.

The trio turned to face the speaker. Before them, standing regally and with a commanding presence, was none other than Lady Arngrim.

————

She was as Holly and Adrian had first seen her; looking like a noble lady from the eighteenth century, resplendent in her white wig, gown and pearls. Of course, the cousins had seen her true form and were not fooled by her appearance.

"Lady Arngrim," said Adrian.

"Do *not* let her touch you," Holly said to Ethan. "Trust me. She is not a friend."

"Adrian and Holly. Of Colchester and Boston. Delighted to see you again, my dears," Lady Arngrim said, sounding at once both light and false. "You left our little party so early, I felt quite bereft of your presence. So rude," she said with a laugh. "It just wouldn't do, children, it simply would not. I just *had* to find you.

"Imagine my surprise when I sensed your presence in the spirit world once more! You really must tell me how you manage to cross over and back like that. I should dearly love to know," she said, and the last bit sounded more like a demand than her previously polite tone.

"We're not telling you anything, hag," said Holly. She said as an aside to Ethan, "Don't tell her anything, not even your name! Believe me, it's for the best."

"Ah, but surely this must be… Ethan Clarke? The boy you were looking for while we were at luncheon." She smiled sweetly. "I never forget a name, dears. It would be most uncommonly rude."

She advanced toward them. They slid sideways as a group, Holly and Adrian guiding Ethan toward the mirror in the corner. It shone bright silver in the light; their only escape, if only they could keep Lady Arngrim from guessing their plan.

"I am most delighted to see you again, children, for not only do you carry within you the bright, warm essence of life—yes, and a heady brew it was, tasting you both as I have—" ("Gross!" said Holly.) "—but now I can sense you have something else, something *more*, and I confess I think I should quite like to taste that, too.

"For you see," she continued as she drew closer and they edged ever nearer to the mirror, "I feel that whatever it is that makes you special will give me the power I need to cross back into the land of the living. To live again! Ah! For that I would devour a dozen, a *hundred* children! And now, it is time! Your light! *Give it to meeeeee...!*" she shrieked.

All at once, she transformed; gone was the noble countenance of the lady, instead was the dark-eyed hag, the banshee who wailed and clutched at the children with bony, clawlike hands.

"The mirror! Run!" Holly yelled. Gone was the pretence of being subtle, as they pulled Ethan to the mirror and placed their hands on it.

Their hands met cold glass; nothing happened.

"The house is still holding us!" Adrian said, panicked. "I don't know what to—"

Holly screamed.

Lady Arngrim had seized her wrist, and Holly was struggling to pull away from her iron grip. It seemed to Adrian that the silvery light in the room was growing stronger, while Holly seemed to grow weaker the longer Lady Arngrim maintained her grip on his cousin.

Ethan bravely shouted "Oi! Let her go!" and began to try to pry the ghoul's hands from around Holly's wrist—but instead found himself grabbed by her other hand, which made him cry out. "It's *freezing*," he yelled.

Desperately, Adrian looked around the mirrored bedroom. Panicking, he flung everything he could at Lady Arngrim—toys erupted from the packed boxes and struck her; these she ignored, her bone-white face grinning, skull-like, in triumph.

Adrian dug deep inside himself and screamed—and the bed rose up off the floor and struck Lady Arngrim, wrenching her grip from Holly and Ethan and pinning her against the opposite wall.

"The mirror, Holly, push it open! Like a door! Force it!" Adrian said.

Holly looked at the mirror, lost. "I-I don't know how," she said.

She and Adrian looked desperately at one another. Adrian glanced over at the shrieking Lady Arngrim, who was struggling to free herself from the bed that restrained her.

"I can't hold her," Adrian said, fearfully. "She's too strong."

"I don't know what we can—wait! Wait wait!" said Holly. "If I find the door, maybe you can push it, we could sort of…join our powers? I do the seeing, you do the pushing?"

Adrian nodded. "We'll only have one try. As soon as I let go of that bed she's going to be over here, grabbing us!"

"Then we'd better make it a good one," Holly said.

Ethan looked confused. "What're you two on about? What is happening?"

Adrian said, "Ethan, when I say, just put your hand on the mirror. Okay?"

"A-all right," Ethan said, clearly not comprehending the why of it but willing to accept direction, given the circumstances.

Adrian grabbed Holly's hand. "Go, Holly," he said.

Holly did her best to ignore the noise and chaos around her, focussing only on the mirror. The world receded from her and she felt the wall—more like a closed door, she realised. And it was the house that was holding it closed. She kept her attention on the door in her mind's eye, holding it there, holding it in the moment—

"Now, Adrian!" she yelled.

Adrian pushed with his mind. Holding Holly's hand, he let go of the bed holding the banshee trapped, which resulted in a shriek of victory from the hungry ghost.

Picturing a door, Adrian could almost feel it—could almost imagine a door being held closed—and screamed as he pushed with all his might.

"NOW!" he yelled, as all three of them put their hands on the mirror.

All at once they lurched forward, falling to their knees in Ethan's room. Sunlight—real, warm, bright sunlight—shone through the windows. They were back in the real world.

But Holly's attention was elsewhere. She was looking into the mirror, and she saw Lady Arngrim, angry and starving, drawing ever closer to the mirror's surface, her face frozen in a scream.

"Adrian, I can see her—she's coming through the mirror!"

"Move away!" Adrian said, and pointed. The mirror tilted forward, toppling over and smashing to pieces on the bedroom floor. The echoes of a shriek died away as it broke, trapping Lady Arngrim on the other side.

There was silence. The trio caught their breath, their hearts slowing to calmer, more reasonable rhythms.

"Are—are we back?" Ethan asked.

Adrian stood, and helped the other two to their feet. He looked out the window at the sunny view of the Clarkes' garden. "See for yourself."

Ethan looked out the window with glee. "We're back! We're really, truly back!"

Adrian exhaled. "For which we are all truly grateful."

Holly looked around, as if listening to something only she could hear. "Can you feel that? The house—it feels happy."

Adrian thought a moment, then said: "Of course. It's not alone any more."

Holly's mouth opened in surprise. "Do you mean—?"

Adrian nodded. "The house wanted company, now it has it. You might even say, the Manor has its Lady once more."

Chapter 10: The Reunion

"Let's just be fabulously where we are and who we are. You be you and I'll be me, today and today and today, and let's trust the future to tomorrow."
—Jerry Spinelli

"Let's get out of here," said Ethan. "I don't want to stay in this house a moment longer."

"I completely and utterly agree," said Adrian with feeling.

"Me three," Holly nodded.

The three children left the room, trotted quickly down the stairs and out the front door, where warm sunlight greeted them. This time, nothing tried to stop them.

"Oh, it feels so good to have sun on my face," said Ethan.

"Me too," said Adrian. "Though even the rainy days of an English summer would be welcome, just so long as we aren't trapped in a spirit house."

Holly sighed. "You can say that again."

Ethan was silent for a while. Then he turned to Adrian and Holly and asked, "What are we going to tell our parents?"

It was the question they had been dreading since exiting the graveyard. How does one excuse an inexplicable overnight absence?

"I was going to ask," Adrian said. "Where are your parents, Ethan? They weren't here last night."

"Oh. We're staying at an inn nearby, so that the house can stay proper for showing while we try to sell it," answered Ethan.

"That makes sense. And I can only assume Mum went home because there was nothing else she could have done," Adrian mused. "Unfortunately, that doesn't solve the problem of what possible excuse we could have for vanishing the way we did."

It was Holly who suddenly brightened. "Okay. I have an idea. We'll probably get in trouble but at least it's believable."

"What is it?" asked Ethan.

"We tell your mum that you were sad about moving so you ran away. We saw you lurking in the trees by the graveyard and tried talking to you, but you were upset, so we spent the night with you calming you down, trying to talk you into coming back, and you finally saw reason and so here we are!"

Adrian frowned. "Why didn't one of us come back to say we'd found him?"

Holly immediately had an answer: "Because he said he'd run away again if we told on him."

Adrian nodded. "It could work."

Ethan also agreed. "I mean, it's not like we could tell the truth. No one would believe it."

Holly sighed. "That's right. Trust me, I know."

Ethan looked at her, then at Adrian. "I just want to say—I know there's something strange about you two. First you stepped through a mirror to find me, then you threw tables without touching them—yes, I saw you." He pointed at Adrian.

"Then there's a ghost and you knew all about what it wanted," he said to Holly.

"Well—" Holly began, trying to think of something that sounded reasonable. This was the part she hated most; people finding out what she could do and thinking it was weird.

"I want you to know that I'm very glad you saved me and it doesn't matter what you did or can do, just that I'm really grateful you did it," he said. And he gave them each a hug.

"But," he mused, "out of curiosity…do you think you maybe have special gifts because you're twins?"

Adrian and Holly both looked surprised. "We're not twins," Adrian said. "We're cousins."

It was Ethan's turn to look nonplussed. "But…you're identical. You look exactly like each other, well, except for the eyes, and by the way you're the first person I've ever seen with yellow eyes," he said to Adrian. "But you and Holly look like brother and sister."

The "twins" looked at each other. "I don't see it," said Holly. "Me either," said Adrian.

"Well, whatever, I'm still so thankful to you both," Ethan said.

Just then they heard the noise of a car approaching. Ethan looked up, and his face froze. "It's my mum," he said.

Holly sighed. "Here we go," she said.

———

All things considered, the plan went relatively smoothly: Mrs. Clarke was too relieved at Ethan's return to be properly upset with him, and when she heard that Adrian and Holly were the ones that convinced him to return, she explained on their behalf to Adrian's mother (who had driven furiously over to the house when Lydia rang her on the telephone), which forestalled Mrs. Whitingham's wrath, and instead watered it down to mere frustrated annoyance.

"You could have rung me or something," she chided Adrian, with some asperity.

"I don't have a cell phone," Adrian said. "You said it wasn't a priority."

"Oh!" said his mother in exasperation. "Well. I suppose all's well that ends well, but we are going home and you two are going to stay there," she said, with an "I don't know what else to do with you" look on her face.

"Suits us!" the two cousins said in unison.

———

The rest of the summer was "delightfully normal," as Adrian put it. He continued to show Holly around Locksley Hall, and she helped him in the garden (not least by speaking for Tom the gardener so Adrian could hear his advice), and Adrian practised his telekinesis when they were alone together.

Holly, for her part, had started writing in a travel journal her mother had bought her for the trip. "I think diaries are silly and girly and I hate them," she said, "But a journal about stuff that actually happened is more grown-up and I think it's important to remember what we learned," she said.

Adrian agreed. "What if someone reads it?" he asked.

Holly shrugged. "They'll think it's just a story I made up. Face it—it's too weird for anyone to take seriously. I'm calling it *'Holly's Book of Stuff,'* so it's not like anyone would be interested in it anyway."

Adrian laughed. Then he sobered. "I meant to tell you—I rang Ethan yesterday, just to see how he was getting along. I tried asking him how things were, but it seems he doesn't remember anything about what happened to him! He says he just ran away from home but we know that's not what really went on—it's like he's completely forgotten everything; he barely remembers me at all."

Holly nodded. "I wondered if that would happen. When normal people see weird stuff, they tend to ignore it. But if they're forced to deal with it, their mind does this protective thing where they do their best to forget it ever happened.

"It's a defence mechanism, I think, to prevent people from going all doo-lally because they saw something upsetting. I'm actually kind of happy for Ethan—who'd want to remember being trapped in a lonely house?"

She paused, thought a moment, then resumed:

"I also have been thinking about Lady A a lot, and I wanted to warn you: remember how I said ghost places aren't connected? That ghosts can't just go wherever they want, because the fog stops them? There's actually an instance where that doesn't apply: it's called a 'haunt.' If a ghost is haunting an object or a person, they can follow that person or thing around wherever it goes. They're kind of tethered to it, connected to it."

Adrian swallowed. "That's disturbing. What are you saying? Lady A is trapped in the house, isn't she?"

Holly made a wry face. "That's just it. She touched *both* of us. She said she sensed us in the spirit world. She found us inside Ethan's house, even though it's not her place. Remember how she sensed we had something 'extra' to us? She's got a taste for our 'special proper magic,' as you put it.

"It's possible we might be haunted by her—by which I mean, that she can find us if she ever manages to get out of Ethan's house. Just keep your eyes peeled—I mean not like you could see her, but if you ever find that the room gets cold, or the hairs on the back of your neck stand up, or you feel tingly all over—those are signs that a ghost is near. Just be careful, okay?"

Adrian suppressed a shiver. "Well, that's just great," he said sarcastically.

Holly nodded. "I know, it's not the best situation ever."

They said nothing for a moment.

Then Adrian said: "I'm going to really miss you when you go home."

Holly's face fell. "I've been trying not to think about that. I finally found someone cool who understands stuff, even the weird stuff, and he lives halfway across the world."

"It's not as bad as all that," Adrian said. "There's the internet. We can email and video chat. Even when I'm away at school there are computers I can use."

"Same here," Holly said. "And maybe after this summer your parents will let you have a cell phone."

Adrian shrugged. "Also a possibility. See? Saying goodbye doesn't have to be hard."

But it *was* hard. Even as the summer came to a close, both cousins felt such a strong connection with each other that, as Adrian waved goodbye to Holly as she and her parents boarded the train, tears were shed by them both.

However, they both had something to look forward to; next summer, it had been promised that Adrian would visit the Weavers in Boston for the entirety of summer vacation.

"I am so looking forward to seeing your place," Adrian said.

"I am literally counting the days," Holly said as they said goodbye.

As the train pulled away, Adrian wiped his eyes and waved, seeing his "twin" getting further away, and his thoughts were already on when he would see her next.

"Shall we have cream cakes at Fortnum's?" his mother asked.

Fortnum's was Adrian's favourite tea shop, and did the very best desserts.

"Yes, please!" he said, cheering up somewhat. His mother took his hand and led him to where her car sat waiting.

Chapter 11: Epilogue

"The future is not something we enter.
The future is something we create."
—Leonard I. Sweet

Adrian sat in front of his computer, in the library at school, reading the emails between him and Holly.

A soft breeze blew through an open window, making him shiver as the hairs on the back of his neck stood on end. He looked around, but saw nothing out of the ordinary.

He exhaled slowly. "Well, great," he said to no one in particular.

END OF BOOK ONE